JOE AND ME
A LOVE STORY OF A GUITAR AND HER BOY

CAROLYN AYRES

STANSBURY
PUBLISHING
Chico, Ca.

Joe and Me
A Love Story of a Guitar and Her Boy

Copyright © 2021 by Carolyn Ayres
ISBN: 9781935807667 paperback
ISBN: 9781935807674 ePub

Library of Congress Control Number: 2021940225
First Edition

Cover art by Carolyn Ayres

Stansbury Publishing
An Imprint of Heidelberg Graphics
Chico, California 95928

Acknowledgements

My friend, Sylvia Hedlind, encouraged me to enroll with her in an Osher Lifelong Learning Institute (OLLI) writing class led by Velda Stubbings. Without that invitation *Joe and Me* would not have come into being. Thank you, Sylvia (and husband, Gary, who gave some excellent feedback on the manuscript). I began the book under Velda's fine guidance and leadership, and finished it with another writing group—Six Meet. These five intelligent, hilarious, excellent writers kindly edited my manuscript through many changes. Thanks to Jim Smith, Neil McCabe, Martha Roggli, Dennis Wilson, and Miklos Sajben. I love you all!

To the Reader:

This story is filled with musical terms—un-understandably. It is the story of a guitar. You will notice these words as they come up throughout the tale. However, there are a few you may want to review ahead of time, because they are used either as puns or in some other playful manner. (Example: In my dismal downward *glissando*.... or .... a rapid *crescendo* of unbearable events....) By reading them now, you are more likely to recognize their double meanings when they show up. The two examples above are related to the actual meanings of the musical terms. However, many of the ways these words are used have nothing to do with their meanings. (I was worried and began to *fret*.)

Amp: An amplifier
Allegretto: In a fairly brisk tempo
Allegro: In a brisk tempo
Andante: In a moderately slow tempo
Arpeggio: The notes of a chord played separately in succession
Beat: The tempo or rhythm of a piece of music
Clef: Any of several symbols placed at the be-

ginning of a staff, indicating the pitch of the notes written on it

Chord: A group of notes sounded together

Compose: Create a work of art, usually literature or music

Crescendo: A passage of music that gradually increases in loudness

Cut time: The beat goes twice as fast

Dampen (guitar strings): Reduce or stop the vibration of the strings of the guitar

Decibel: Relating to electrical signals or sound intensities

Diminished chord: a chord that is lessened by a semitone

Double time: Twice as fast

Falsetto: A method of voice production used by tenors to sing notes higher

Glissando: A continuous slide of adjacent notes upward or downward

Grace note: An extra note added as an embellishment

Home key: The key a song begins and ends with

Key: The letter name given to indicate the pitch the song will be played in **Minor scales or minor keys:** The third note of the scale is lowered a half step, giving a sound often interpreted as spooky or sad

Note: A single tone of definite pitch made by a musical instrument

Perfect pitch: The absolute pitch of a note

Pitch: The degree of highness or lowness of a tone

Repeat sign: A sign that indicates a repetition of what has just been played

Scale: An arrangement of all the notes in a system of music in ascending or descending order

Sharp: Above the normal pitch

Staccato: Each sound sharply detached or separated from the others

Tempo: The speed at which music is played

Tenor: Singing voice between baritone or alto; or the singer with this voice

Timbre: (pronounced tamber) The distinct character of a musical sound or voice

Tone: A musical sound

Treble: High pitched

Tremolo: A tremulous effect made by rapid reiteration of a note

Guitar Words

Catgut strings: Strings for guitar made of sheep intestines

Fret: Bars or ridges on the fingerboard of a guitar

Grain (wood): The texture of wood

Tuning pegs: Used to tighten or loosen the strings on a guitar

Strings: The guitar has six strings made of steel or nylon; historically, made of "catgut"

🎼 ♪ Chapter 1

My first awareness of life came with someone touching my back with a tap, tap, tap.

"Ah, what a rich, mellow sound. You are my finest work," I heard a man say. "Welcome to the world, beautiful guitar."

I was a guitar? Cool! But if I was a guitar how did I know this person was a man, and why did I know what he was saying? Why did I know anything?

However, undeniably, I knew things, one being that a guitar wasn't supposed to have consciousness. Curious. What was I to make of this? Did this man use magic? In making me, had he, in essence, put a genie in the lamp? I was completely fascinated.

"I made you special, just for Joseph, my soon-to-be born son." He cocked his head and looked puzzled. "Why am I telling you this?"

I liked that he was talking to me. I didn't want him to stop. If I were a dog, I would have wagged my tail. I tried to wag, anyway. My bottom quivered.

"Holy moly! What was that?" the man exclaimed. "You wiggled!"

Now we were both fascinated.

"Could it be you understand what I'm saying?"

Yes, yes, I wanted to answer.

"I had a dream the other night that you were magic, but what I just saw was no dream." He kept talking. I hung on every word.

"In my dream, I loved you, and I wished you were alive, kind of like in the story of Pinocchio." As he talked, he rubbed my neck. I liked it! My strings made a purring sound.

The man jumped. "Whoa! Did you just vibrate your strings?"

I wanted to laugh. Although it was a strange relationship, we were getting to know each other, and I was having fun.

He placed his fingers on his chin, puzzled. "In case you can understand me, you might want to know this. All the while that I was putting you together, making you especially for Joseph, I experienced a great love and anticipation for his birth. Then one day, something strange happened. Hard to explain, but from my hands, I felt love enter your sides. I didn't think much of it at the time, but after my dream, I'm wondering."

He looked away, and it seemed he was now talking to himself. "Love is a powerful emotion.... maybe strong enough to create miracles." He nodded. "Yes, strong enough to create this miracle." Tears came to his eyes.

I understood everything the man said, so apparently, some kind of magic was taking place. Through his love he had somehow infused me with consciousness.

The man shook his head. "If Collette hears me talking to a guitar, she'll think I've lost my mind." He relaxed a bit, looked at me, and smiled. "It will be our little secret."

Using the pegs that were sticking out of my head, he tightened a few of my strings. It felt as if I were stretching—ahhh, I loved the feeling.

"Let's see how you sound, my magical guitar." He began strumming, playing a slow melodious tune that was so incredibly beautiful, I wanted to cry.

When the song ended, the man said, "Amazing! I've never heard such beautiful sounds coming from a guitar." He pointed. "See the guitars hanging on the wall? I've made them all, and not one can match the sound I just brought from you."

Although I had not heard the other guitars, I had to agree that I sounded amazing.

"You are the perfect guitar for Joseph. He won't have a brother or sister, because Collette and I are too old to bear more children, but you will be Joseph's companion." He rubbed my back. "When he is old enough, I will give him lessons. Then when people hear him play, they will say,

'Where is that angelic sound coming from? I've never heard anything so beautiful.'"

While I sat on a guitar stand throughout the rest of the day, I was full of curiosity, eager to see the unborn child this man loved—the boy who was the reason I was alive; the boy who was to be my companion.

I didn't have long to wait. According to the calendar on the wall, it was January 7, 1933, two days after I came into the world, that Joseph was born. I knew, because from somewhere upstairs, I could hear a high-pitched squall. Intermittent crying and screaming went on for a number of days and nights.

It'll be awhile before I want to be this child's companion, I thought. Nevertheless, I was impatiently curious, and finally, on the sixth day, Collette brought the baby to the workshop.

"Victor, come talk to our little Joseph." Victor went over and began murmuring unintelligible words to the crying baby. The two of them beamed as if the discordance were sweet music. What was I missing? I could only detect irritating screeches and wailing.

For the first few months after Joseph was born, I rarely saw him, but I often heard him, sometimes cooing and babbling, and other times exercising his vocal cords at a high pitch.

From the guitar stand, I could see a staircase that led up to where I assumed the family ate, slept and lived. I was left alone each night in the dark workshop. I didn't like it. I was surrounded by other guitars—beautiful, but lifeless. They brought me no comfort. As the dawn came, I listened expectantly for Victor's footsteps. When the stairs creaked with the sound of his boots, my spirits brightened. He always greeted me in one way or another, usually by rubbing my side and talking to me.

"Good morning. How is my magic guitar?"

Sometimes I joyfully wiggled my bottom, letting him know how happy I was to see him. After greeting me, he would begin another day of cutting, molding, filing, and bending wood into beautiful guitars.

One day I looked at Victor closely. He wasn't exactly a head-turner until he smiled. When his warm eyes lit up and crinkles formed around his mouth, his face became irresistibly good looking. A small bit of gray peeked out from a full head of curly black hair. He had a short, tidy beard and a distinctive nose on which hung a pair of round-rimmed glasses. All in all, I liked the way Victor was put together. I liked the way Collette was put together, too. Her hair was black like Victor's, but it was shoulder-length and straight. Her soft brown eyes and red lips could stop a guitar in mid-arpeggio.

On my stand, as I watched Victor work, I pondered the gift he had given me. Not only was I alive, I didn't have to start out with an empty slate. I had an unexplainable wisdom. In this way, I was not like a newborn child who needed to learn everything through experience and maturing. And, of course, I was not like any of Victor's other guitars either. They were what was to be expected—inanimate, inert objects. I glowed with aliveness. I could feel it. Victor had created them to be beautiful, but they didn't know they were beautiful. I knew I was, and that is what separated us.

One day when Collette came down to the shop, Victor was listening to Mozart on his phonograph. He told Collette that Mozart played his first composed piece on the piano when he was four and that he wrote his first symphony when he was eight. I related to Mozart. We were both inexplicable surprises to the world.

After a couple of years passed, Joseph began his journey through the "terrible twos." When things didn't go his way, he threw himself on the floor, banged his head, kicked and screamed. If he wasn't in the workshop, I could hear his head and feet thumping on the floor above me. I recognized the connection we had with each other as I paralleled his behavior by going out of tune or breaking one of my strings.

14

When Joseph crawled down the stairs backwards to be in the workshop, the two of us fed off of each other's energy.

One day he pointed at a small saw and said, "I want dat, Papa."

"Sorry, son. It's too dangerous. You will hurt yourself."

Joseph stomped and screamed. "Gib it to me, Papa."

That set me off and I popped two strings. These were some of our first bonding experiences.

Although sometimes obstinate with his parents, Joseph was always incredibly gentle and sweet with me. One day he rubbed his little hand up and down my side.

"Do you like that guitar, Joseph?" Victor asked.

"Yes. It pwetty."

"I made it for you. When you get bigger, you can play it."

Joseph rubbed my side again.

"That part of the guitar is made of rosewood," said Victor.

"Wose," said Joseph. "I wike you, Wose."

From then on, Joseph began calling me Wose and later, Rose. I began thinking of him as Joe instead of Joseph.

Joe was in that young part of his life where things were not separated into animate and in-animate. He talked to everything—his shoes, the tools in the workshop, bugs, me. When he got older, and things began to separate into living and nonliving, I remained in the living category. Victor and Joe often included me in their conversations, treating me as the live entity that I was.

 Chapter 2

As *Joe got older,* he continually followed Victor around asking if he could help. Victor tried to include him when he could.

"Here, Joseph. I've made a small hole in this piece of wood. See if you can twist a screw into it with the screwdriver."

Victor held the screw as Joe turned it, his little tongue curled up on his lip to help him concentrate.

As they spent time in the workshop together, Victor talked to Joe about the guitar.

"What do you think this is called, Joseph?"

"Silly. Dat the side."

"Yes, and it has another name—ribs."

"Wibs? Dat funny."

"Let's find your ribs." Victor put his fingers under Joe's shirt and poked around. Joe giggled.

"Dat tickles."

"Your ribs keep your body from collapsing."

"Coll—what?"

"Collapsing—caving in. The ribs on the guitar do the same thing. They keep the top and bottom apart."

"I tickle Wose's wibs, Papa."

As Joe ran his fingers up and down my side, my strings vibrated—not exactly a giggle, but close.

Joe put his hand on a different part of me.

"What dis, Papa?"

"That's the bridge. It holds the strings in place."

"Look, Papa. My fingers are walking acwoss the bwidge." Then he put his fingers on my sound-hole. "Why does Wose have a heart? The other guitars have circles."

"When I was making Rose, I was thinking of you, Joseph. You weren't born yet, but I felt so much love for you, my hand shaped the sound-hole into a heart, almost without me thinking about it."

With Victor's words, my hollow insides glowed with a great love for him. Not only did he use his hands to make me magical, but by forming a heart for my soundhole, he created a way for me to love. At that moment, I understood just what an unusual creation I was. I wanted a mirror so I could get a good look, see a reflection of the unique, magical, loving guitar that I was.

On another day, Joe put his hand by the tuning pegs. "What dis part, Papa?"

"That's the head of the guitar. Your head sits on your neck, and Rose's head sits on her neck."

Joe plucked one of my strings.

"You call dis stwing, but Mama has stwing and it don't wook wike dis."

Victor laughed. "You might as well know that the strings of the guitar are made of catgut, but they're not from a cat. They're from a sheep—from the intestines. A gut string is made from the intestines—the guts—of a goat or sheep."

"Ew! Yuck!"

"Yes, pretty yucky, but much stronger than your mother's string."

Joe plucked one of my strings again. "You have a lot of guts, Wose." He laughed at his own joke. Then he ran his hand across all my strings. "Am I big enough to play the guitar, Papa?"

"Your hands are still too small, son. Be patient. The time will come."

Sometimes at bedtime, Victor would carry me to Joe's room to sing lullabies. If I was lucky, I got to stay while either Victor or Collette read fairy tales. I loved them all: *Rumplestiltskin, Cinderella, Sleeping Beauty, Hansel and Gretel, Little Red Riding Hood*, and, of course, *Pinocchio*. Because of my own magic, I related easily to these stories. I would have been comfortable being a character in any one of them.

One day when Joe and I were seven, Victor was gone from the workshop. Joe took me off the stand, banging my side against a stool as he carried me to the worktable.

Careful, Joe.

He awkwardly hoisted me onto the bench and climbed up on the stool beside me. With a nearby screwdriver, he removed the screw from the gear connected to my top right tuning peg. It fell into a crack in the floor and was gone. My body quivered as I began to panic. Would I start falling apart?

"Hold on, Rose. I'm going to fix it." Joe climbed down, hurried over to a container of screws, chose one, climbed back up, and with some difficulty replaced the one that was lost.

Ahh. Much better.

Later that day, when Victor returned, with gentle loving hands, he picked me up and began to play, then stopped abruptly.

"Joseph, one of the silver screws has been replaced with a gold one. What do you know about this?"

A gold screw? Joe put in a gold screw instead of a silver one? If I thought of my tuning pegs as ears, I could pretend I had one gold earring. *Cool! Don't change it back, Victor,* I silently pleaded.

"Yes, Papa. I was working on the guitar like you do, but I lost the screw, so I found another one." He jumped up and down. "I helped make a guitar!"

Victor smiled. "We can leave the gold screw there to show that you helped make this guitar, Joseph, but Rose must stay on her stand until you are bigger. We would both feel bad if she got hurt."

My days were enjoyably spent, sitting in the shop, watching Victor work. He had music playing constantly, either from the local radio station or from his phonograph. From the radio, I became familiar with Cole Porter, Ella Fitzgerald, Bing Crosby, Jimmie Rodgers, Tommy Dorsey, Glenn Miller, Louis Armstrong, and Duke Ellington. Victor used the phonograph to play classical music. My favorite composers were Mozart, Beethoven, Tchaikovsky, and Chopin.

One day a young man, maybe twenty, tall and thin, with long blond hair, entered the shop.

"Hello. Are you Victor Marcini?"

"Yes, I am."

"I am Jake DeGarma. I would love to have a look around. I've heard about the Marcini guitars."

"Jake DeGarma? The folk singer?"

"Yes. That's me."

"Quite an honor, Jake. Please take your time."

I watched Jake move from guitar to guitar. As he strummed each, he cocked his head, listening to the tone.

"Beautiful, Mr. Marcini. These guitars are exquisite!"

Then he spied me in the corner. His eyes lit up. What could I say? Victor had made it clear that I was the most beautiful guitar in the shop.

Jake picked me up, appeared to look at the one gold screw and then turned his attention to the rest of me. As he began to play, I resonated with a pure

vibration that filled my hollow insides with joy.

"I must have this guitar! What are you asking for it?"

What? Leave Victor and Joe? Go live with someone else? Please, no!

"I'm sorry, Jake," said Victor "That guitar is not for sale. I made it for my son, who will play it when he's old enough."

Neither of them saw my relief, but the disappointment on Jake's face was noticeable. A short while later, he purchased one of the other guitars, thanked Victor, and left. The danger had passed. I sat the rest of the day feeling relieved and grateful for the homey, warm place I lived, and for the people who adored me.

Each day Joe came by and dragged his fingers across my strings.

"Please, please, Papa. When will you teach me?"

At long last, on Joe's eighth birthday, Victor took me from my stand, pulled up a chair in front of the fireplace, and said,

"Come sit with me, son. It's time."

🎼 ♪ Chapter 3

The day I had been waiting for was finally here. Victor had told me when Joe played me, I would make angelic sounds—sounds that would make people stop and listen in amazement. I couldn't wait!

In the first lesson, Joe watched carefully as Victor demonstrated the fingerings for the D and A7 chords. He played the melodic D chord first, switched his fingers to A7, a chord with some dissonance, and then back to the D chord again, a sweet resolution. I loved the sound these two chords made when played in relationship to each other, and I loved the way Victor's fingers felt on my strings.

"With your fingers holding down the strings, strum back and forth like this as you switch between the two chords."

With Victor's guidance, Joe placed his fingers on my strings in the D chord formation as he strummed his right hand across the strings. He changed to the A7 chord and strummed again. The two of them worked on both chords for a while, Victor exhibiting great patience, and Joe doing his best to hold the strings down.

When Joe strummed, the two chords sounded nothing like when Victor played them. I became edgy. I felt like I was being tortured. I tried to squirm out of Joe's hands.

"Hold still, Rose," Joe said. "What's the matter with her, Papa?"

"She is not used to you playing her," Victor said. "But as you practice, she will settle down."

At the end of the lesson, Joe thanked his dad and then wasted no time in taking me to a chair in the corner. With a flourish, fingering the D chord, Joe hit the strings hard. As the discordant clash erupted, I almost leaped out of his hands. This was not the angelic music Victor promised. Joe moved his fingers to A7 and strummed again. My E string broke and curled up like it had been electrocuted.

"Daddy!" yelled Joe. "Something happened. One of Rose's strings broke."

Victor came over, removed the broken string and replaced it.

"Rose doesn't like to be played by a beginner," said Victor. Turning to me, he said, "But all great guitar players were beginners at one time, Rose. I know you will soon become adjusted to Joe's practice sessions."

I was certain I would soon be maladjusted as Joe practiced! I didn't know if I could endure it. Victor created me with the best materials, using his expertise to bring about a guitar with a magical sweet sound, unmatched by any other. I had heard those sounds many times as Victor played me. I took them for granted. Who would have guessed I could now sound so bad?

Through the following days, to make Joe stop, I loosened or tightened my strings as he played, but it didn't work. Joe got frustrated with me, but he wouldn't quit.

"Rose, you need to stop that. Daddy, can you come tune Rose again? She keeps messing with her strings."

Victor, ever patient, came and retuned me.

"Hang in there, Rose. It's almost time for another lesson. I can hear Joe's improvement already."

I couldn't. Day after day, the pling, pling, pling of Joe's fingers on my strings were like the drops of a Chinese water torture.

In the lessons of the following weeks, Joe began learning scales, which could not be called music at all. Up and down my neck went the fingers of his left hand, his right hand plucking, plucking, plucking.

Joe often squeezed in a practice before he left for school. One morning I could hear the aggravation in his voice.

"Rose, your strings are so tight, I can't get a good sound. Help me out a little."

I ignored him. He left for school and I reveled in the silence.

I did see that Joe was trying, but he still couldn't hold the strings down tight, so the tones were fuzzy and distorted. My ego was battered each time he picked me up. Clearly, I was only as good as the one who played me, and the one who played me was not good. What a travesty to have my clarity of sound and beautiful tones wasted on a beginner. My potential sat dormant under inexperienced fingers.

But Joe never got discouraged. He came alive with his new passion, and Victor reflected Joe's enthusiasm by walking with a bounce and wearing a continual smile. Strangely, it was the happiest I had seen either of them.

The lessons continued. One day, Victor said, "You have great potential, Joseph. I've not seen anyone learn so fast. Soon your hands will naturally twist in a way that makes it easier for you to hold the strings tight."

I figured Victor was building Joe up so Joe wouldn't feel discouraged with the eternal racket he was creating. Loving, patient Collette, added her own encouragement.

"Joseph, that was lovely. Play it again."
Groan.

To protect myself from ending up in the Looney Tunes bin, I began using my imagination to travel to other places. As the weeks went on, I saw myself in large concert halls with people doing standing ovations after Joe had brilliantly finished his performance. People yelled out things like, "Beautiful guitar!" "Great sound!" "Wonderful! More, more!" Naturally, the crowd would not stop clapping until we did one more song. Since I was imagining, I took it a step further and finished the evening with a flamenco number that I performed without Joe's help. My admirers were back on their feet, clapping and calling out. "I can't believe it. That guitar is magic!" These musings turned out to be a great diversion from the daily practicing that so offended my finer sensibilities.

Interestingly, my daydreaming had become so habitual, I missed the subtle shift from terrible to not so bad. One morning as Joe did his before-school practice, I "woke up" because I heard an angelic, clear chord progression. Glory be, were those sounds coming from me? Yes! While I'd been daydreaming, Joe's guitar playing had turned the corner. *Ahhh.* The tension in my strings eased.

"Rose," Joe said. "You seem more relaxed today. You sound better than usual."

Yes, he was right. Oh joy! I sounded only as good as the one who played me, and the one playing me was getting good!

One afternoon, Collette came into the workshop and said, " You might not get your dinner tonight, Victor. I don't have much energy today."

"I'll come help you, Mama. Just tell me what to do, and I can make the dinner."

Joe put me on the stand and bounced up the steps with his mother following. I liked Joe's sweet spirit. I could see it more clearly now that my attitude toward him had softened.

More days passed and by increments, the resonance Joe brought forth from my wooden body improved. The musical development had moved at a slow andante pace, hardly noticeable, but now the progress was moving in rapid allegretto leaps. The puffy-bubbled blisters on the ends of Joe's fingers had long since turned to rough, hard calluses. He had mastered a variety of strums and riffs, and my strings began to ring pure and clear with the improved strength in his fingers.

I could see that I was coming to the end of a dark tunnel of misery, and back into the wonderful light of day. Had this experience changed me for the better? And if yes, in what way? Had I become humble? No. Had I developed patience? No. If not humility or patience, then what? As the question posed itself, I realized I had inadvertently fallen in love with Joe. Coming out of this troublesome time together had created a bond between us. I wanted to be with him all the time. Also, Joe showed me how tough and determined he could be, a quality that in the beginning, I abhorred, but now admired.

Returning from school one afternoon, Joe said "Hi, Rose." As he took the stairs two at a time, he called over his shoulder, "I'll be right back." He returned with a peanut butter sandwich. While he was eating, some of the messy, squishy filling got on his left hand.

Oh-oh. I objected to having any contact with peanut butter.

Joe laid his unfinished sandwich down and picked me up. I tried to pull away, but as I feared, he smeared the icky goo on my neck. *Ew! Disgusting! Seriously?*

Sticky, gross peanut butter smudged on my smooth, polished neck? Every part of my body retracted.

Joe noticed. "What's going on, Rose?"

He would find out when his hand slid across the greasy, nasty stuff. He began to play, and as I knew he would, he stopped.

He looked down and laughed, "I see. You don't like peanut butter smudges all over your neck."

With a rag, he cleaned his hand and then shined me until I glistened. All spruced up again, and returned to my natural luster, I relaxed. A sigh of delight floated through my heart and tick-led my strings.

Joe smiled. "I see you're happy again, Rose. Sorry about the peanut butter. You're back to your beautiful self now. Let's fill this room with music." He caressed my cleaned silky neck, cradled me in his arms, and began to play. His attitude toward me had changed. Because he no longer struggled, his view expanded, and he recognized me as the magnificent instrument I was, rather than a common practice instrument.

"You sound wonderful today, Rose." Joe stopped to rub my neck again. My sides began to vibrate in a purr, and like a contented cat, I completely relaxed.

Joe resumed playing, but interrupted himself again. "What just happened? You sound even better!" I didn't realize how much my past tight-ening and grimacing had contributed to the poor sounds that came from me. My total relaxation caused a noticeable improvement. I hated to admit it, but through all of those grueling months, Joe was only part of the problem. He had struggled, and I had resisted. By some miracle, the two of us, each with our own dysfunction, had finally moved ourselves from discordant to melodic. Maybe the improvement would have come faster and easier if I had surrendered and tried to help.

While Joe laid me down to finish his sandwich, I thought about this insight. If one person wants to learn the tango, but the partner is resistant, the two may never be a smooth couple on the dance floor. In frustration, the one may finally say, "I give up. Learn it yourself."

Which, of course, would be impossible. To learn to dance the tango or to play a magic guitar, it takes two. One can't do it alone. Thanks to Joe's persistence, he and I finally emerged as a unified twosome.

Still chewing his last bite, Joe picked me up and began again. Heavenly! I sounded so good, I wanted to hear me over and over. Joe stopped and said, "Rose, I love you!"

My memory was selectively short. I forgot what a pain Joe had been and what a grump I was. Shamelessly, I rewrote the story. This version showed that Joe helped me improve what I originally thought was my perfect self. I was now wiser, more mature. In this expanded view of my splendid being, I had always been a team player. Additionally, I bravely withstood the physical abuse, knowing it would strengthen my core, make my spirit indestructible.

However, this tale, true or not, no longer mattered. Through our difficult times, Joe and I unwittingly formed an unbreakable bond. We were in sync, connected. Until my heart opened, letting Joe in, I hadn't realized I wasn't complete.

In the following three months, I looked forward to the daily practices. Joe had mastered the basics. He was flying high, and I was his co-pilot. Practice didn't feel like practice anymore. It felt like pure fun. We were hanging out, jamming together, creating unbelievable music.

One afternoon, Joe went a little crazy—wild and creative. His left hand moved rapidly up and down my neck. The fingers of his right hand were a blur. I became a gyrating wonder. Sounds chimed through my body, ringing, echoing, reverberating. My strings sang to each other, as the rich tones resonated through my heart. By the time Joe finished, he glistened with perspiration.

"Wow, Rose! I'm not sure what happened there. We went a little crazy."

Yes, crazy-wonderful.

 Chapter 4

One day a potential buyer, someone who would change our lives, came into Victor's shop. Joe and I watched as he sat down on a stool with the guitar he had chosen. Along with a bluesy fingerwork, he sang a few short phrases. I watched Joe's eyes light up with pleasure and my whole body began to hum. After the man finished, Joe asked,

"Who are you? I want to learn to play like that."

"They call me Mitch. Mitch Williams. Can you play?"

"Yes," responded Joe. "My dad taught me."

"Show me what you can do."

Joe picked me up, settled onto a chair and began to play. I watched Mitch. At first I could see he was being polite to the son of the famous luthier, but as Joe began playing chords in rapid progression, Mitch sat up straighter, and watched Joe's nimble fingers intensely as they danced up and down my neck.

When Joe finished, Mitch said, "I've never heard a guitar with a more beautiful tone, and you are a gifted player." He was quiet for a moment. "Would you like to be my student? I will teach you to play jazz, and you can learn to sing blues."

I liked Mitch! He had not only said Joe was gifted, but that I had a beautiful tone.

Victor, working at his bench, said, "I know you by reputation, Mitch, and once, a number of years ago, I heard you play in a nightclub in New Orleans."

"Yes. Presently, I'm playing at Mayfield's Jazz Bar."

Victor looked at Joe. "I am proud of what you have accomplished with my lessons, but Mitch can teach you things I can't. It's time for you to sprout new wings."

"I get to learn to play like that?" Joe jumped up and hugged Victor. "Thank you, Papa. I'm going to tell Mama!" Joe ran up the stairs.

Joe and I had just turned twelve. Although I looked the same, Joe had changed. He was tall and thin, some would say skinny. When he nestled me against him, I could feel his ribs bumping against mine. He ate mountains of food, but instead of growing out, he grew up. Sometimes he stumbled over his own feet, probably because he didn't realize their size had changed almost overnight.

It was easier now to see the genetic link between Joe and his parents. Joe had wavy black hair, a combination of his mother's straight and his father's curly. He had Victor's strong hands and nimble fingers—fingers that looked like they were made for playing a guitar. I liked his soft brown eyes, much like Collette's. When Joe gave me his warm smile, the pupils of his eyes got bigger, and from inside, I could see the love. It nearly melted my tuning pegs.

Of course, my own genetic background was much different from Joe's. My ancestors came from Europe and South America. In my family tree was spruce, mahogany, and a Brazilian rosewood. My blond, straight-grain spruce top contrasted with the beautiful and durable reddish-brown mahogany that made up my neck.

The part of my body I loved the most was my back and sides, made of a purplish brown Brazilian rosewood, resistant to decay and insects, and with remarkable acoustic properties. I was sure Victor chose this particular piece of rosewood because it had a unique black streak, called "spider webbing," which formed a grain pattern down my back. Its effect was stunning. All of this would have been enough, but I possessed an added attraction. The rosewood gave me a distinct rose-like scent. Not only did I look and sound good—I smelled good!

Victor took these three woods, and with his unusual skill, created me, an exceptionally gorgeous, beautiful-sounding guitar. Joe and I were two genetic wonders. No one would have guessed by looking at this twelve-year-old boy that he was a child prodigy. Although we came from very different backgrounds, I was also a prodigy—a one-of-a-kind guitar. Together we were prodigious.

Victor began taking the two of us regularly for lessons with Mitch. After each lesson, Mitch picked me up, lovingly stroked my sides and neck, and played me with a look of intense joy on his face.

"This guitar continues to be an amazing wonder," he said one day. "Your father is a gifted guitar maker. If this guitar didn't belong to you, I would buy it in a minute."

Joe got a concerned look on his face. "She will always belong to me. I would never sell her."

This did not surprise me, but still, the words were music to my ears. I liked Mitch. I liked the way I sounded when he strummed my strings, but Joe knew me better—knew how to get the best sounds from me. And why not? We were practically born together. Like siblings, we didn't always agree on things, but we were connected by "ood"—bl*ood* or w*ood*, depending on the point of view.

During this period of time, Victor took Joe on as an apprentice. I watched as Victor guided Joe through the steps of construction, beginning with learning about which wood to use. I watched as Joe learned to make a sound hole, how to bend the side pieces, carve a neck, attach a fret board and put it all together.

One day Victor asked, "Now that you've begun to learn the steps, how are you enjoying building a guitar? Is it something you think you'd like to do in the future?"

Joe's eyes lit up. "Papa, you know how much I love guitars. It's so cool that I get to make them now."

Victor gave a smile. He reached out and gave Joe a warm hug. "Nothing could please me more. Welcome to Marcini and Marcini Guitars."

Two more years went by, and then after one of the guitar lessons, Mitch spoke to Joe. "You've learned so much so fast. You are going to do amazing things with your life, but I won't be here to see them."

Joe blinked. "What are you talking about?"

"I've been doing some gigs in Memphis. I have family there. That's where I'm headed."

I watched as Joe stared at Mitch, cleared his throat and said, "I-I don't know what to say. Good luck, I guess. I'll miss you." He awkwardly stepped forward and gave Mitch a hug. "I feel like I've been the luckiest kid in the world. I'll never forget you."

"Take care of your guitar, Joe. I've never seen or heard another like it. When you play it, the guitar seems to be trying to please you by resonating with a tone I can't get from it." He shook his head. "Okay, forget I said that. It's a guitar, and the two of you make a fine pair."

Mitch could feel my aliveness, my desire to please Joe, but rationally that made no sense, so his logic took over, and the real thing—his experience, got left behind.

As we headed out the door, I wished I could tell Mitch that I would miss him, too. I was starting to miss him right then. I would never again hear him say how wonderful I was. He would not be picking me up and stroking my neck. How very sad.

Little did I know I would be seeing him again....
under ill-fated circumstances.

 Chapter 5

Joe's lessons stopped, but we continued to
create glorious music together. I no longer sat in
the shop. Joe kept me in his room. Our energies
wound around each other—Joe the grapevine, me
the rose. I started knowing where his fingers were
going before he moved them. He began responding to my urgings for a spontaneous change—a
different chord or an unusual rhythm.

As soon as he got home from school each day,
he tenderly wrapped his hand around my neck,
took me from the stand and sat in his chair. I
liked the way his thumb and finger felt as they
grasped my tuning pegs to tighten my strings.
Finished with the tuning, he tucked me to his
side as if I were a perfectly fitting puzzle piece.
As he began to play, I emanated a love-hum that
added an underlying rich, resonation.

"Rose, you sound better every day," he said
one afternoon. "As I improve, so do you."

I knew what he was talking about. Each day
Joe played, we sounded better than the day before.

Collette stepped through the door and said,
"How about you get better at doing your home-

work?" I saw her eyes twinkle as her lips up-turned into a slight smile. "Finish that, and then you can continue to get better on your guitar."

Yes, Joe had homework to do most afternoons when he got home from school. In his English class, he was learning about some of the great American writers. Sometimes while Victor was making guitars, Joe sat and read to him—poems by William Blake and Walt Whitman.

One day Joe read aloud from *Walden's Pond*. I became enamored with Thoreau as I discovered how much he liked trees. Because my ancestors were trees, I felt a kinship with him. Thoreau thought trees had a mysterious quality and were able to "see" beyond themselves, as social networks.

On this subject, Joe said, "Yes, Papa, my teacher said that researchers are starting to find evidence that trees communicate with one another. They have intelligence."

I was hanging on every word.

"This doesn't surprise me," said Victor. "I've always thought trees have a seeing and hearing that doesn't require eyes or ears."

This explained a lot. I was made up of tree parts. Although I had no eyes or ears, I could see and hear. Victor had inadvertently activated the tree consciousness that was ingrained in my wood.

Joe continued. "It's probably the same intelligence that a spider uses to make a web, or a seed to root and become a tree."

Joe and his dad talked on, but I was no longer listening. My own thoughts were swirling with this explanation of my own intelligence. I was connected to a vast web of aliveness and perception. Victor had invested me with the wisdom found in all of nature, showing up in my wooden parts as a genius Mother Earth IQ. I was filled with a bubbling joy about who I was—this wonder Victor had created.

At various times throughout the following weeks, prompted by homework assignments, Joe and Victor had similar philosophical discussions. The two of them had such an easy and open way of talking to one another that it made listening in on their conversations a pleasure.

Life was good, wonderful, fantastic. I couldn't imagine anything finer than my life as it was, nor could I imagine that our joyful childhood would end. Like me, Joe was happy most of the time. It was not until two years later that the tenor of our days shifted downward and off-key.

Joe was finishing up his homework when Victor said to him, "Your mother is not feeling well. Ask her if she wants you to play for her."

Joe and I quietly entered Collette's room.

"Mama, what's going on with you?"

"I'm having trouble breathing, and I have no energy."

Joe's brow furrowed. "Maybe I can make you feel better. Last week I wrote a special song for your birthday. I think I should play it now."

Joe's arms gently circled my body and we began to fill the room with music. As he played, I could feel him using the music to calm his own fears. When we finished, Collette said,

"Joe, that is the best gift...." She took a long, deep breath ".... the best gift you could have given." She began coughing and when she finally stopped, her energy was spent. As she sank onto the pillow, she closed her eyes.

Two days later, Joe returned from school, lifted me from the stand and we went to Collette's room again. We didn't play that day, though. The room was dark. I could hear wheezing, as Collette's lungs struggled for air. Joe bent, gave her a kiss on the cheek, and we left. In the kitchen, Victor was talking on the phone.

"Doctor Thomas? Yes. This is Victor Marcelli. My wife, Collette, is very sick. She is having trouble breathing."

Victor paused, listening.

"Yes. She has a fever of 103 degrees."

Another pause.

"Thank you. We're on our way." Victor hung up and turned to Joe. "Your mother took a real downturn today. I'm worried."

"Me, too, Papa. I'm glad you called the doctor. I'm going with you."

Joe took me to his room, put me on the stand, and left. I could hear Victor talking to Collette.

"My dear Collette, Joe and I are going to help you to the car. Dr. Thomas has cancelled one of his appointments so he can see you. It will take us forty-five minutes to drive into New Orleans. Do you think you can do it?"

In her raspy voice, Collette said, "Thank you, Victor. I will do my best."

When the front door closed, I was left in the quiet, empty house, feeling like a broken chord.

Two and a half hours later I heard the car's wheels crackling on the driveway. They were back. As the three of them entered, I heard snatches of conversation.

"... pneumonia ... must watch ... fever ... penicillin." And then Victor's voice came through clearly, "I hope it's not too late."

I began to tremble. *Too late for what?*

Joe entered the room, took me to his chair and began to tune my strings. After a couple of tries, he said, "Rose, I can't get you in tune." He paused. "You're a wreck, aren't you?"

Yes, I was a wreck. I wanted to cooperate, but I couldn't focus.

"I'm a wreck, too. Let's see if we can make ourselves feel better."

He tried to get a lively piece going, but I kept slowing it down. With my whole body stressing, I couldn't put my heart into it. Joe gave up.

On a Monday, in the early morning, rain began to tap on the roof. As it came down harder, I heard another sound, muffled by the storm—Victor, moaning and crying in the other room. Soon it awakened Joe. He jumped out of bed and ran. Above the sound of the rain, which was now coming down in torrents, I could hear heart-wrenching crying from both of them. I knew Collette had died. The realization that I would no longer have her in my life broadsided me. My hollow center felt a different kind of empty, an empty that was dark and deep, where no light could enter. I wanted Joe to play me, to soften the ache, but I sat on the stand in his room all day. As the rain continued, its gloom moved into the house. I numbed myself to the sounds of the coroner as he came and went.

In the late afternoon Joe finally came to the room, but he laid on his bed and stared at the ceiling. I wanted to play him a tune to cheer him up, but without his fingers, I was just a piece of hollow inert wood with six strings.

As the days passed, the rain stopped, but the gloom remained. Hal, a friend of the family, came to the house. I heard him talking with Victor, making plans for the funeral.

Each day following the service felt like an eternity. Joe and Victor moved aimlessly around the barren house, not speaking, their grief palpable. I knew Joe wasn't going to school, because he never left the house, and from what I could tell, Victor wasn't making guitars. Joe stared out the window or laid on his bed. Victor must have been doing the same. Even though there were the three of us, the house felt empty—empty and joyless.

One evening Victor came to Joe's room and paused at the door. Joe stood, and the two fell into each other's arms. Joe began heaving with sobs while Victor rubbed his back. Not until that moment did I realize that my catgut strings were also heartstrings, plucked for the first time when Joe began to cry. They played a song I'd never heard before, the most heartbreaking song imaginable. The sadness moved into my body and I began to quiver.

Joe pulled away from his dad, turned and looked at me like he'd just noticed I was in the room. He paused a moment and then put his hand on my spruce top.

"Rose, you are feeling our pain, too." He must have sensed my heart's agonized pulse. "I'm sorry—sorry for you, sorry for us."

Victor spoke. "I will bring another guitar so we can play and sing together to lighten our hearts." He left and returned with a guitar I had heard him play many times—one not of my excellence, but still, a fine guitar. Joe put me in his arms, and they began, father and son, singing "O Solo Mio." They closed their eyes and played with the feeling that the song engendered. Victor sang melody, Joe the harmony. I contributed by fully relaxing my strings so Joe could get a full tone from them. All that existed was the music.

> ... *But another sun,*
> *That's brighter still*
> *It's my own sun*
> *That's in your face!*
> *The sun, my own sun*
> *It's in your face!*
> *It's in your face!*

I saw my own sun in the faces of Victor and Joe. My heart felt lighter.

One morning, a few days later, Joe got up, left the room, and came back with wet hair and a towel wrapped around him.

"Rose, I'm going crazy, thinking about Mama. I'll be better off at school."

After Joe left, Victor came in, took me from the stand, rubbed his hand lovingly over my top and side, and began to play. He sang in a beautiful bass voice a song Collette had loved: "Ma L'Amore No." His voice cracked on the last verse, but he finished the song.

But love, no
My love cannot
Dissolve in the hair's gold
Till the end, love will remain alive in me
Just for you.

Then he cried. I thought my wooden heart would shatter into splinters.

♪ Chapter 6

I was relieved the morning I heard Joe speak easily to Victor.

"Good morning, Papa. How are you doing?"

"Oh, Joseph. I'm walking around each day like I haven't got a soul. I know time will help, but right now it's hard. And you? How are you faring?"

"Same as you, Papa. Letting the time pass."

A couple of weeks went by. One morning, I watched Joe get his clothes on and grab his books. His footsteps took him to Victor's room.

"Get out of bed today, Papa," I heard him say. "Go make guitars. It will help the time pass more quickly."

"Yes. I'll do that. Thank you."

With Joe's bedroom door open, I could usually hear most of what took place in the rest of the house. And if I listened intently, I could even hear fainter sounds from the workshop below.

That morning, Victor did get out of bed, but instead of hearing pounding and sawing, I heard the dialing of the phone.

"Hal. This is Victor. I want to thank you again for your help with Collette's funeral. You have been a steady, dependable friend through the years." A short pause, and then, "Say, I'm wondering if you can come over. I need your advice on something." Another pause. "Well, one thing is that I'm having trouble breathing, and my chest feels heavy, like something is sitting on it. I'm worried. I don't know what's going on. Maybe it's my heart. My father died of a heart attack." After a pause, he said, "Thanks. It will be good to see you and we can talk."

His heart? Something was wrong with his heart? My own heart began a nervous tremolo.

Later there was a knock on the door and Victor's welcoming words.

"Hal! Thank you for coming. Let me make some coffee."

Clattering in the kitchen was followed by scraping of chairs. Victor began talking about his symptoms.

When he finished, Hal said, "I think you need to see a doctor, Victor."

"Yes, I'm thinking the same thing. But I've also invited you over for another reason."

Their voices lowered to a pianissimo. I could hear snatches of what they were saying, but I couldn't make sense of it. Victor murmured, "Joe ... help with ... cared for ... conservator."

Then Hal's voice, "Your finances. ..."

I'm naturally nosey. I wanted to know everything that was being said. What were Hal and Victor whispering about? Although I loved being a guitar, it had its limitations ... no sneaking up and listening from behind the door.

After a while, chair legs scraped again. I heard Hal ask, "How are you feeling at this moment, Victor? Would you like me to take you to the doctor now?"

"No, no. I can take myself. I'll see if I can get an appointment for tomorrow."

"Maybe you shouldn't wait. This condition seems serious."

"Thank you, Hal. Maybe I'll see if I can get in to the doctor today."

"Yes. Please do. Let me know what he says."

But after Hal left, instead of hearing Victor pick up the phone, I heard the creak of footsteps going down the hallway and into his bedroom. After what seemed like hours of silence, I heard the front door open. My heart began a jumpy staccato beat. Joe was home from school!

"Hi, Papa," he yelled as he came through the door. "Where are you?"

"In here, Joseph. I'm not feeling well. I'm rest-ing."

This time it was not a creaking sound I heard in the hallway, but thumping footsteps shaking the floor down to Victor's room.

"What do you mean, Papa? What's wrong?"

"I'm having a little trouble breathing. I'm going to rest for awhile."

"Trouble breathing? Do you have pneumonia like Mama?"

"No, no, son. It's nothing like that."

"Shouldn't you go to the doctor?"

"Yes. I'll go tomorrow."

"Can I do anything for you? Are you hungry? I can fix you something to eat."

"Thank you, Joseph. You're a wonderful boy. Nothing much. I'm not too hungry."

Joe seemed quick to give his father the love he himself had received so abundantly as a growing child. I had also received love from Victor—while I was being made, and also in the years following. I wanted to give, too, but the only thing I had to offer was the soothing sounds I could make, and I couldn't do it alone. I hoped Joe would think to come get me, but he didn't. He kept talking to Victor.

After years of sitting for hours on a stand, one would think I had learned to wait. But no. I still had the patience of a ukulele. I wiggled myself off the stand and hit the floor with a clatter.

Joe was by my side immediately. "Rose! What are you doing? You could hurt yourself." He carefully picked me up and rubbed his hand over my neck and back, examining me for damage. Then he cocked his head to one side, and said, "Oh, I see. You want to help, too."

He brought me into Victor's room.

"Rose wants to make you feel better. We'll play a song before I get you something to eat."

I put my whole self into creating a slow vibrato while Joe's tenor voice crooned "O Solo Mio." Victor smiled with so much love I could once again feel my sun in his face.

The next morning, not too long after I heard the door close behind Joe, I heard it open again. Hal walked quietly past Joe's bedroom door. There was a knocking and Victor's voice.

"Yes?"

I heard Hal push the door open. "It's me, Victor. I'm worried about you. Did you get in to see the doctor yesterday?"

"No, I decided to rest."

"Do you have plans to go today?"

"Yes, but I haven't called yet."

"I'm taking you in now. You are as pale as a ghost."

Soon they shuffled past me and out the front door. I was left alone to brood. My neck and back tightened until they began to hurt. In desperation, I prayed—something I'd never done before.

Please, please let Victor be okay. I need him. Joe needs him. He is everything to us. He is Joe's papa and my papa, too. He is a generous and good man, who still has much to offer the world. Please let him be all right.

In the early afternoon, a car drove up. I recognized Hal's footsteps as he came through the door into the front room. I heard him squish down into the easy chair, and then for an hour, I heard nothing. What was going on? Where was Victor?

The squeaking of the door hinge let me know Joe was home.

"Hi, Hal. What's the matter? You don't look so good."

For awhile, Hal didn't answer, and then,

"I came to take your Papa to the doctor this morning. He died of a heart attack on the way." There was coughing and then broken sobs.

Joe's voice was panicky. "It's not true. It can't be true. I talked with him this morning before I left for school. He can't be dead."

Through broken sobs, Hal said, "I'm sorry, Joe. He's gone."

The door slammed, and I knew Joe was gone. Hal left shortly after.

🎼 🎵 Chapter 7

I sat reviewing my life with Victor. His strong love for his soon-to- be born child was the source of the magic and life he brought to me through his hands. I thought about the great love he had for his wife. It was clear to me that his heart attack was really a broken heart.

I wondered what happens to guitars when they die? Would I ever be with Victor and Collette again? I knew guitars can live much longer than humans. Would Joe leave me, too? A sad slow andante vibration moved through my hollow body.

Joe returned late that night. He climbed into bed, but turned one way and then the other, not able to sleep. I watched the whole night through, wanting to comfort him, but I might as well have been a post for all the help I was.

In the morning, I heard him on the phone.

"Hal? Hello. Do you think you can make the funeral arrangements? I'm not thinking too clearly." Silence, and then, "Thank you. Your friendship means a lot."

In the following days, Joe did not go to school. He paced—in his room, in the hallway, in the front room. He wailed, he spit angry words, he pounded his fists against the wall, he cried.

I wanted to comfort him, and also be comforted by him. It would relieve the tension and sorrow for both of us if we played music together, but when my heart called to him, something he could often hear, he was too wrapped up in his pain to notice. We each grieved alone. When I thought about the great sadness that had come into this house, I felt that deep dark emptiness again. As before, my heartstrings began emanating a silent sorrowful, anguished strain of music.

In the afternoon of the fourth day, Joe came into our room, turned to me and said, "The funeral is over, Rose. People will be coming to the house. Let's play some music for them."

A joyful hum filled my lonely heart. I felt like a puppy dog, who cares only about the immediate attention of her owner. I wiggled my bottom, sore from sitting so long.

Joe carried me into the front room and sat on a stool in the corner. He whispered, "Let's do our best."

With sad eyes, Hal greeted people at the door. Joe nodded in acknowledgement as they entered, but focused on me. We began with something we learned long ago from Victor— "La Puesta de Sol." Joe closed his eyes and sang softly in a way that musically carried the song through both of our hearts. Once again, we were entwined as one. The way his fingers plucked lightly on my strings, playing Victor's haunting melodic tune, sent tingles up my back and neck.

Joe sang soulfully throughout the next couple of hours, using me to bring out the poignant beauty of each melody. The whispers and low voices faded as I focused on doing my best for Joe...and for Victor.

After everyone left, Hal turned to Joe. "This is difficult for me, but I need to share some bad news with you."

"Nothing could be worse than what already is. I'll be fine." He looked directly at Hal. "Just tell me."

"A number of years ago, Victor made me conservator of his property. Recently, I met with him to draw up a will. He left the house and all his handmade guitars to you."

"That doesn't sound like bad news to me," said Joe.

"No, it doesn't, but I've been meeting with Victor's creditors. It appears he has been going into debt since long before Collette died. He kept the information from all of us. He was gifted as a guitar maker, but not as a financial planner. I don't think he knew just how serious his debt problems were."

"Exactly how serious?"

"I'll need to have someone appraise the house and the value of the guitars. I fear everything must go to pay the debts."

What? Hal was talking crazy. Don't let him do it, Joe.

As if he heard me, Joe yelled, "No! You can't sell this house. And you can't sell the guitars.

My father put hours of love and care into making them. You can't sell them!" Joe choked and began to cry.

Hal took him in his arms and in a soothing voice, said, "This is all too much, too soon. I want you to come stay with me until other arrangements can be made. I'm sorry about all your pain and loss. No boy should have to suffer like this."

I got scared. No guitar should have to suffer like this! One horrible thing was coming rapidly upon the heels of the next—a rapid crescendo of unbearable events. Would Hal sell me with the other guitars? One thing was certain. No amount of money would be enough to pay for what I was worth. *I am a priceless, one-of-a-kind, never to be replicated guitar!* I tried to compose myself, but I was so upset, my strings began pinging against my neck.

As soon as Hal left, Joe said, "Rose, we have to get out of here. They're not taking you away from me."

My relief was immediate. We weren't going to be separated! I felt myself loosen up. Joe took me down to the shop and dug out my case, which I'd ridden in when we went for lessons with Mitch. I wasn't fond of being shut away, but I'd put up with whatever was needed so we could stay together.

Darkness was immediate. I heard the clamps lock me in. I always felt a little claustrophobic in the case, but I focused on my love for Joe, and my tension eased. I heard him running up the stairs, probably to get those things humans need—a backpack to carry food, clothing and any money he could find lying around. His footsteps clunked back down the steps, but instead of leaving, I heard him walking around the shop. Maybe he was saying goodbye to the guitars, and in that way saying farewell to Victor. I heard him sniffle.

Please, Joe. Let's turn toward where we're going, and leave the sadness behind.

Joe responded to my silent plea. His step quickened. I felt myself being lifted from the floor, and although the case jostled against Joe's leg, I was snug and safe inside. On that note, we left. The door opened and closed and I knew we were in the open air.

If I'd known what lay ahead, I would have been trembling in my case, but I was with Joe and happy, blissfully ignorant of what was to come.

Chapter 8

I was in the moment, living our escape. I came so close to going the way of the other guitars that I was experiencing a sweet, buoyant relief. As Joe walked, fear was communicated with every rapid, jerky step. His nervousness whipped me out of the present and into the future. Spikes of fear struck my frets, the physical seat of my worries. Where were we going? Where would we stay?

Soon I could hear the whizzing of cars and trucks. The road was wet from a recent storm and I heard the wheels splash on the pavement. Joe stopped. What was he doing? My strings tightened. If only I could see! I heard a vehicle stop and a door open.

"Hi, Kid. Where ya goin'?" a scratchy voice said.

"Into the central part of New Orleans," Joe said. "If you're going anywhere near Mayfield's Jazz Bar on Bourbon Street, that's where I'm headed."

"Sure, hop in," the man said. "I'm Richard. What's your name?"

"Joe, and thank you very much." Joe hoisted me into the back seat and clambered into the front. My claustrophobia climbed up a notch. I wanted out so I could see this guy. The idea of me watching out for Joe was ingrained. We were a team. If something went wrong, I couldn't help him physically, but Joe was tuned to my vibes. I could warn him if something wasn't right.

For what seemed like quite a few miles, Richard drove in silence. I relaxed, and being in complete darkness, I dozed.

Richard's loud voice shocked me awake. It seemed he had been thinking of other things, and then realized he had a passenger.

"What could you possibly want with a jazz bar on Bourbon Street? That's a rough section of town. How old are you?"

"Eighteen," Joe lied.

We had both turned seventeen just last month.

"Why that bar?"

"I had a guitar teacher once, who played there in a jazz band," Joe responded. "Mitch Williams. He's up in Memphis now, but I want to see the place."

"Mitch Williams? Really? He's well known in these parts. Wonderful jazz singer. How did you meet him?"

"My father. He was a luthier."

"Was? What is he now?"

"Dead." Joe's voice was flat. "He made beautiful guitars." I could hear Joe choking up. He cleared his throat and continued. "Mitch came to buy a guitar, heard me play, and offered to give me lessons."

"So are you some kind of a good guitar player now?"

Joe didn't answer immediately. "Yeah. I'm okay."

That's one of the ways Joe and I differed. I wanted the world to see how great I was. Joe was modest. He would show you what he could do, but he wouldn't brag about it. Modesty was an endearing quality, but not one I could relate to. My beautiful wood and mellow sounds all but shouted, "Notice me." We complemented each other. I was hard to his soft, short to his tall, hollow to his full, flamboyant to his modest. Rose and Joe, yin and yang. My greatness allowed Joe to shine without him having to sell himself. I did that for him. If people were to hear us, they'd fall in love with me. They would start wishing I was theirs. "You have a beautiful guitar," they would say. Yes, there was no denying it. I was gorgeous, and I was what made Joe great.

"I play some guitar myself," Richard said. "Show me what you can do. It is your fare for the ride."

"Really?" I heard trepidation in Joe's voice. "I don't think there's enough space in here for me to pull out the guitar. You know, you can just let me out and I will find my own way."

When Joe said that, I knew he realized something wasn't quite right with this guy.

"Now that's no way to return a favor," Richard spoke roughly. "I insist. Let's hear you play."

"I'd rather not."

Richard shouted. "What's with you? You don't have a choice you scrawny freak. Play!"

I began to tremble. I heard the fasteners click. Light flooded in as Joe opened the case. He was on his knees, bending over into the backseat. He wiggled me around to pull me out and then carefully lifted me to the front.

Ahhh! Light. Fresh air. ... Oh gag! Not fresh air. Richard was smoking! Disgusting! And was that alcohol I smelled on his breath? We were in trouble.

I saw that we were nearing the center of New Orleans. Besides houses, there were a few restaurants and stores with cars parked near them. We could make it on our own now, but how could we get out of the car?

Joe tuned me and together we gave Richard a slow sad song. Joe's voice sagged on the notes. I dampened my strings, which produced a fuzzy sound. We were not about to put on a stellar performance for this thug.

Richard said,"Your guitar is a beauty. I think it might have to be your payment for the ride."

Joe sucked in his breath and did what I had wanted to do. He gave a primal howl. It sounded like a drawn out "Noooooooooooo." Richard reached out to grab him and Joe did something I would never have expected. He sank his teeth into Richard's arm! As far as I knew, Joe had never been in a fight. The bite was clearly a terrified instinctual act to preserve the one thing he had left in his life—me.

Richard howled with pain. While trying to shake his arm free, he lost control of the car and it went careening to the side of the road, hitting a parked car. The abrupt stop caused Richard to bang his head against the side of the car. His body slumped over the steering wheel. Joe and I were thrown against the door, but it seemed we were both okay.

Joe didn't wait. He opened the door, held me tight by the neck while he grabbed his backpack, and we bolted. There was no time to get the case. After covering a distance of a couple of blocks, Joe was panting, and I was beginning to get a sympathetic side ache. I know I slowed him down, but even so, he soon put a great distance between Richard and us.

As Joe eased up, my tight body did the same. Our escape was impressive. With unrehearsed clarity, Joe had acted quickly and courageously in the moment. He was my hero.

As we moved toward town, I experienced an after-shock realization of our close call with Richard, and I shivered. I shivered again, remembering we were completely on our own. Joe and I had left all stability in the past and were walking on new ground where we did not know what would happen next. Our home in the peaceful outskirts of New Orleans was a place where neighbors knew and cared for each other. Now alone and vulnerable, all we had was each other. What was it like in downtown New Orleans? Would we have to guard and protect ourselves from everyone we met?

Fear churned deep in my hollow belly.

Chapter 9

With Joe's hand securely wrapped around my neck, we moved down the road. The bustle of the city began to show up as the streets became more clogged with cars. Some were parked along the streets, a few yellow, blue, or red ones among the mostly black. I saw people of many colors—various light-skinned ones, and brown ones, all the way from light to very dark. They sauntered along singly, or in groups of two or three, chatting, looking in the store windows, not in a hurry. Joe slowed his own pace, moving in step with the others.

Nearing a crossroad, a tall dark-skinned man opening his car door turned and smiled at us.

"Nice guitar you have there. Looks like you could use a strap."

"You're right. I need to get one."

"I recently bought a new one for my guitar. I have the other here in the car. Let me donate it. You don't want to be bumping that beauty around. It's way too nice."

Just like that, with no strings attached, this stranger gave up a guitar strap. His thoughtful words caused the tension of today's events to ease. My taut strings loosened. Nothing like being noticed and appreciated to turn the murky cloud enveloping me into a disappearing mist.

Joe gave him a big smile. "Thank you, sir. You are very kind. I will get it put on right away." He looked down the road and then back at the man. "I wonder. Can you point the way to Bourbon Street?"

"Yes," the man answered. "You're almost there." He gave directions, and handed Joe the strap.

"Thanks again," Joe smiled.

"Good luck," the man said, and climbed into his car.

As Joe and I moved in the direction of Bourbon Street, he said, "The kindness of a stranger has given me a good feeling about this place, Rose."

It was late afternoon when we entered Bourbon Street. Glowing street lamps overtook the fading sun. I was mesmerized with their soft reflection on the wet pavement. As we walked, we passed a corner grocery store, two tailor shops, a sandwich shop, a two-story brick building with a "For Rent" sign, a jewelry shop, and a number of restaurants and bars. From one of the bars, a tantalizing jazzy blues floated through the air. I was hoping Joe would stop, but he looked straight ahead, focused on finding Mayfield's Jazz Bar. Further along, I heard more music—saxophone and piano, along with singing. Bursts of laughter mingled with the notes. These people were having a good time. After the sadness Joe and I had experienced, I felt a longing to be a part of it.

We had come into New Orleans many times for Joe's guitar lessons, but that was during the day. The dusk brought with it a feeling of expectancy, suspense, a growing energy. A group of young boys passed us talking excitedly. The delicious smell of food wafted through the air—not something that interested me personally, but I could feel the excitement and anticipation of those entering the restaurants. I felt alive, amped up.

We were into the next block when Joe said, "We've found it, Rose."

Sure enough, there was Mayfield's Bar, with big neon letters announcing itself. When a couple walked through the door, Joe took a deep breath and said, "Here we go," and we followed them in. I was so excited, I almost burst at my glued seams. We were going to see where Mitch played! But wait. Would they let us in? Joe was not yet eighteen.

The room was dimly lit with people sitting at a weathered, pocked bar. My strings wrinkled up from the smell of old wood, stale cigarette smoke, and sour beer. Through an open window behind the bar, I could see the kitchen and a bald man, who I guessed was the cook. In this dark cavern was a stage with piano and drums, and below, a wooden dance floor surrounded by tables of different sizes, all covered with white tablecloths. A few people sat, drinking beer and eating.

A burly man with a reddish beard and upper arms the size of bongo drums stood behind the bar.

"Can I talk to the manager?" Joe asked.

"He doesn't talk to little kids," the bartender responded. "You'll have to leave."

I didn't like this man's tone.

Joe talked rapidly. "I might not look it, but I am eighteen. I once took guitar lessons from Mitch Williams. I understand he used to play here. I would like to try out for the band."

A booming laugh erupted from the bartender. After he settled down, he said, "Do you think because you took lessons from Mitch you can come waltzing in here and take his place?" He turned to someone at the bar. "Do you hear that, Jimmy? We have the next Mitch Williams in the house."

Jimmy looked over. "Does he have his mama with him?" He laughed. "Where are you from, kid?"

Joe did not answer, just frowned.

The bartender rubbed his chin, looking at Joe. "What I could use is a dishwasher. It's not the job you came in for, but it's the one I'm offering."

Still frowning, Joe looked off in the direction of the stage. I knew getting a job washing dishes was not what was on his mind when he walked through the door. If only the bartender knew how incredible we were. We needed to demonstrate.

It occurred to us at the same time. Washing dishes was a foot in the door. Joe turned back and looked directly at the bartender. In an even, polite voice, he said, "Thank you, sir. I would like that."

A twinkle came into the bartender's eyes. I realized he was not as much of a grump as I thought. Not thinking Joe could be much of a guitar player, maybe he was amused with his bravado. "You start tomorrow. Show up at 4 p.m."

We turned and went out the door.

Joe had a job! It wasn't the job he wanted, but it was a job—a way to survive in this unfamiliar city. But where were we going to stay tonight? My emotions were on a roller coaster.

We moved along until we came to the brick building we'd seen earlier with the "Room for Rent" sign. Joe knocked on the door, which was directly in front of the sidewalk. Seconds later a dark-skinned woman wearing a gray dress with a white apron answered.

"I'm interested in renting a room," Joe said.

"How old are you? I can't take minors."

"I'm eighteen, ma'am."

"I hope you ain't lyin' 'bout your age. It's $3.20 per night or $20 a week."

"I have enough to pay for the first week. I just got a job at Mayfield's Jazz Bar, so I should be good for the rest of the month's rent once I get paid."

The woman showed us our room on the second floor, small with a single bed and one curtained window, looking out on Bourbon Street. The bathroom was down the hall, shared with other tenants.

Joe paid the landlord, thanked her, and we entered the room. After he shut the door and sat on the bed, Joe did something unexpected—he began to cry. Of course he cried! I wanted to cry, too. It felt like a hundred years since this afternoon when we left the house. We each held it together all day, but in the room with nothing else pressing, the truth settled in. We were now completely alone in the world.

I wanted to comfort Joe, but I could only lie on the bed with him, feeling sorry for myself, and even sorrier for him. We had only each other. Could we survive? I wasn't sure.

Chapter 10

The next morning, Joe took a towel and left the room. I presumed he was going to take a shower, which was a good idea. He stank. I had a built-in perfume—the lovely smell of rosewood and spruce. Joe, however, was reeking of second-hand cigarette smoke along with some unidentifiable odors. Let's just say our smells were not harmonious.

While Joe was gone, I began to fret. I wondered, "*What will Joe do with me while he goes to work? Leave me on the bed? He has a key to the door, but the lock seems rickety. If people know I am in the room alone, what's to prevent them from breaking in and stealing me? Maybe Joe will hide me under the bed. Perish the thought! That would be worse than spending the day in a case.*"

I should have known better than to worry. When Joe returned, he ate an apple and a chunk of cheese from his backpack, and then said, "I have to figure out how to take you to work with me, Rose." He picked me up, grabbed the guitar strap and we went down the stairs and out into the street. Passing businesses and restaurants, we eventually came to a music store.

As we entered, a bulky man with black hair and mustache asked, "May I help you?"

"I wonder if you can put this strap on my guitar."

"Certainly. It looks like you could also use a guitar case."

"Yes, but I'll need to wait on that. How much to put on the strap?"

"I can do it for a quarter."

"Thanks. That would be great, and one more thing. I need some kind of hook that I can hang my guitar on."

"Ah. I think I have something you can use. Let me look."

Immediately I saw what Joe was up to. He planned to take me to work and hang me on a hook where he could keep an eye on me while he was washing dishes. If I had legs, I would have jumped for joy.

While the man was looking for the hook, we moved around the store, seeing saxophones, drums, a stand-up bass, a piano and lots of guitars. I tried not to be judgmental, but really, none of the guitars came anywhere near my splendor. I was a long-stemmed Rose among a field of dandelions. If they had any life in them at all, they would be experiencing jealousy, but they hung there, unaware. Jealousy was not an emotion I would ever know. What guitar could compete? Not only was I gorgeous, I had someone who talked to me and stroked my neck; someone who knew how to play me in a way that brought out my rich musical qualities. No, jealousy belonged to those who did not know their own worth.

Just as the store man returned with the hook, a man and young boy who looked to be twelve, entered.

"My son needs a guitar. He wants to learn to play," the father said.

The store man said, "Take a look around. I'll be with you in a minute."

I watched as the father and son went from guitar to guitar. If I were hanging on that wall right now I would be cringing. I knew what it was like to be played by a beginner. Like in *The Three Billy Goats Gruff*, I imagined one of the guitars saying, "No, no, not me. Please take this one next to me. She is much more beautiful."

My attention returned to the store man, who was picking me up and carrying me to the back. I was terrified. I knew what happened to guitars that had straps attached. Holes were drilled in their bottoms! I wanted Joe there, assuring me I'd be all right.

Before I knew it, the deed was done. The man affixed one end of the strap to a bright shiny button and tied the other around my neck above the top fret. Although it was a used strap, a beautiful design was woven into it—a perfect accessory for my beautiful self. I felt like I was wearing a Miss America banner. The man didn't notice my spruce top puff up with pride. He wouldn't have, anyway. People don't see things they don't believe in, and few believe in magic.

When we returned to the counter, Joe paid, and the two of us left, with me riding on Joe's back. While he saw where we were going, I saw where we had been. We had Bourbon Street covered.

🎼 ♪ Chapter 11

We *showed up* at Mayfield's Jazz Bar a few minutes early. The men at the bar turned their heads as we entered.

The bartender spoke. "What are you doing with the guitar? I thought we talked about this yesterday. You're a dishwasher."

"I'll keep the guitar out of the way. It won't be a problem."

In the kitchen, Joe found a nail hole near the door, away from the steamy dishwater and greasy grill. He screwed in the hook and up I went. It was a perfect observation post. I was thrilled. The squat, bald-headed man I saw yesterday through the bar window, stood over a stove, wearing what used to be a white apron. He smiled, and grunted a greeting in our direction, then went back to scraping the grill. A young waitress came through the kitchen door. She had what seemed to be naturally red lips and rosy cheeks. Her long taffy hair was pulled back in a ponytail.

"Hi. I'm Emma. I'm the waitress here. You must be the new dishwasher." She smiled. Joe nodded. "Glad to have you" she said. "The last one quit a couple of days ago, and it's been tough."

"Well, I'm Joe. I'm glad I can be here to help."

Emma's blue eyes sparkled. "Believe me, so am I. Washing dishes while also waitressing is a bit much." She pointed toward the sink. "Most of your time will be spent keeping the dishes washed up, but when you can, you will also help me set and clear tables."

"Thanks, I'll do my best."

"Dinner is served from six 'til ten. Right now, we can get the dining area set up."

After finishing in the dining room, Emma whispered, "Don't let Abe's gruffness bother you. He has a soft heart."

"Who's Abe?"

"The bartender. He's the head honcho here."

"Glad to know. I haven't seen the soft side of him yet, but he did give me a job." Joe smiled. "I guess he can't be all bad."

A short while later, a tall, lanky kid rushed through the kitchen door, breathing hard.

"Sorry I'm late, George. Put me to work." He pulled up beside Joe. "Hi. I'm Rupert. You the new dishwasher?"

"Yes."

"Cool! I'd much rather chop vegetables than do dishes." He put his hand out and they shook. "Glad you're here."

The cook and his assistant began chopping and sauteing food. A menu hanging nearby was titled French Creole. At the top of the menu was something called gumbo. Other foods included red beans and rice served with ham hock and pickled pork; and dishes with oysters, shrimp, and crawdad. Soul food.

Music was my soul food. For the evening customers, eating gumbo while listening to a New Orleans jazz band—ahh! Soul food on many levels.

At five, I heard shuffling and clattering from the stage area. With the boom-boom of a drum, and the sound of a saxophone doing some warm up scales, I knew the band was setting up. If dinner was at six, why were they here so early? As I listened, I knew. They were rehearsing. Besides the drums and saxophone, I could hear a piano, a bass and a guitar. I could also hear arguing.

"Roy, when I play this line, your guitar is doing something that is completely off. Can't you get it right? We've been over this lots of times."

"Get off my back, J. T. What I'm playing is exactly right. You're the one who is off."

As they rehearsed, arguments continued. J. T., who I determined must be the saxophone player, seemed to be the leader. I could hear two singers. I knew one was J. T. because the saxophone always stopped when he sang. I wasn't sure, but I thought the other might be Roy, the guitar player.

Something about Roy bothered me. I hadn't actually seen him, only heard his voice, but when he spoke, a foreboding started my body trembling. What was wrong with me? I felt like I was being silly, but I couldn't shake my uneasiness.

To get myself thinking in a different direction, I took in my surroundings. This was not going to be a boring life. Besides what was going on with the band, there were other things to keep me occupied. I was able to listen to Joe and Emma interact as they did their jobs. I could hear laughter and good-natured bantering from the bar. The cook was his own show, wielding his impressively sharp knife, a tool that made me slightly nervous. I hoped a finger didn't end up in the gumbo.

Did I hear him humming while he chopped? Yes, humming and singing. He obviously relished what he was doing. Since a creator cannot be separated from his creation, I suspected he prepared heavenly food that made people happy. This same thing happened with Joe and me when we played our music. The joy we felt was contagious, and so made others happy.

I wished we could provide happiness to others right now—giver and receiver in a mutually happy loop. My head jerked with a stab of impatience. It was hard, hanging on the wall, watching Joe scrub and polish, something that could be done by anyone. The unique music we played could be done only by us. When would we be able to play our music for others?

Joe tuned into my thinking. "Patience, Rose. We'll get our chance. Right now I'm a dishwasher, but we'll find our way onto that stage."

Joe always said the right things. He kept me grounded. My strings relaxed.

I knew it must be six o'clock when I heard a commotion from the front door. Along with the scuffle of feet and the click of high heels on the wooden floor, I heard laughter, greetings, and a general hubbub of activity.

I heard Emma's sweet voice ask, "Would you like to be seated near the music?"

"Yes. That's why we're here." A small laugh. "And the good food, of course."

The band began playing while Emma seated the guests. I settled back against the wall, anticipating the evening of music. The band started right up. Emotion flooded my body as I heard the sonorous sound of the saxophone. J. T. was a master! The piano player's ability to weave his harmonies around the single horn melody was almost too beautiful to bear.

At the time, Joe was pulling glasses from a shelf. He looked up and said, "I can see you like the music, Rose. Pretty wonderful, huh?"

Emma had just entered the kitchen. "What did you say? Were you talking to me?"

Joe gave a short laugh. "No, just mumbling to myself about how much I like the band."

"I know. It makes working here not so bad."

They smiled at each other, which made me all warm and tickly inside. Above all, I wanted Joe to be happy. I provided a kind of happiness for him, but he needed human companions, too.

The only thing that dampened the rest of the evening was Roy's guitar playing. He didn't always choose the right chord. Also, he strummed when he should have picked, and picked when he should have strummed. His level of expertise didn't measure up to that of the other players. However, I was jaded, and so not the one to ask. It was hard for me to be content with any guitar music other than my own—as performed by Joe, of course.

A couple of weeks went by like this. Without complaint, Joe washed enough dishes to fill a concert hall. Then one afternoon, during rehearsal, J. T. stepped off the stage to get a drink of water. He poked his head into the kitchen and said, "Hello, Joe. I notice you have a beautiful guitar hanging there on the wall. Do you play?"

Joe left his dishes and came to stand right under me. He glanced up at me and said, "She is beautiful, isn't she? And yes, I do play."

"Sometime, you'll have to show me what you can do."

"I'd like that very much." He cleared his throat nervously, took a deep breath and said, "Since we're here talking, maybe it wouldn't be too presumptuous of me to make a suggestion for Roy and that song you're having trouble with."

"Not at all. Fire away," said J. T.

"If Roy flatted the five in the third chord of the bridge to get it to tie in with the sax line, I think it would all come together."

"I understand exactly what you're saying," said J. T. "We'll give it a try." He looked back over his shoulder as he left. "You obviously know a little about music."

I wanted to jump down off my hook and give J. T. a big hug for listening to Joe and respecting his knowledge. Maybe this was the beginning of something bigger. Back at the stage I heard J. T. talking to Roy. When the band played through the bridge, I could hear the improvement. The music stopped and J. T. yelled, "Thanks, Kid. That was it. We've got it now." Speaking to the band, he said, "Okay, let's take it from the beginning."

Joe had a smile on his face as he went back to washing dishes. Emma walked up to the sink and said, "That was impressive, Joe. Who are you? How do you know so much about music?"

"Oh, I play some guitar myself, as you would suspect, from seeing my guitar hanging here." He pointed and smiled.

"Yes, I've noticed. Beautiful. Where did you get it?"

"My papa was a famous luthier. He made this guitar especially for me."

"How did you learn to play it? From your papa?"

"Yes, he taught me first. Later, I took lessons from Mitch Williams."

"Wow! Really? I was hired to work here just before he left. He packed this place!"

"Yeah. I was sorry when he moved."

Emma left with silverware for the tables.

"She's kind of cute, don't you think, Rose?"

Well, what do you know! Joe was sweet on Emma. I suspected it with the smiles I'd seen. From the recent pain in Joe's life, he carried a sadness inside. Emma's kindness was what he could use a lot of right now.

A few days later, during rehearsal, I heard J. T. griping at Roy again.

"There's something very wrong about what you're doing on that line, Roy."

"I'm sick and tired of this," Roy complained. "I'm telling you, my part is fine. You need to fix what you're doing."

Joe had stepped out the kitchen door and was listening to the argument. I heard J. T. say, "I'm interested in hearing what you have to say about this part of the song, Joe."

"Thanks. I was listening, and I think if you used a diminished chord that ascends while the bass player descends, you'd like the sound."

"Leave. Right. Now. Before. I. Throw. You. Out," Roy said. Joe quickly retreated, which I thought was an excellent idea.

"Let me try that diminished chord on the piano," said another voice.

"Thanks, Sam," said J. T. "Let's try it."

They began the song again. Upon reaching the part that hadn't worked, the piano and bass carried it and the piece came together.

"That's it! I'm glad I said something," Joe said out loud.

Emma said, "Careful, Joe. Roy seems explosive. Maybe you should stay out of it."

I was thinking the same thing. I didn't want anyone messing with my boy.

Although he had been rude to Joe, I felt sorry for Roy. He did some things well, but his repertoire of chords and musical understanding was limited. How difficult to be playing with musicians so much better than he was. I suspected the loud posturing was a cover-up.

When his shift was over, Joe lifted me onto his back and walked toward the front door. Blocking our way was a guy with narrow-set eyes and unkempt brown hair. He stood with arms crossed and legs apart. Although scrawny, he was quite imposing.

"You better be minding your own business, punk, or I'm going to tell Abe lies about you, and he'll kick you out on your ass."

So this scary guy was Roy. I no longer felt sorry for him. I clenched my strings.

"I don't understand why you are so mad."

"We don't need a kid acting like he knows everything, telling us how to play our music. You think you're some kind of a hot shot, but you're a dishwasher. Don't forget it." Roy stepped aside and shoved Joe through the doorway. "Stay in the kitchen where you belong."

𝄞 ♪ Chapter 12

In the following days, Joe and Emma became better friends. They talked and laughed easily. I could see Joe taking sidelong glances, watching Emma as she moved around the kitchen. She had her eye on him, too—and no wonder. He was close to six feet tall, had black wavy hair, warm brown eyes, and his killer smile was enough to make any girl stop in her tracks. However, the greatest appeal came from inside: his kindness, his strong sense of self, and his modesty.

I was glad Joe had an admirer. I knew the feeling. From the time I came into this world I had admirers. Like Joe, I was a feast for the eyes and had a strong sense of self.

One day in the kitchen, Joe asked, "Where is your place, Emma?"

"My mom and I live in an apartment not far from here. How about you?"

"Same here," said Joe. "Well, I don't live with my mom, I live with my guitar." They laughed.

"Nearby," he added. "You want to meet up some-time for a walk, before we come to work?"

"Sure. How about tomorrow? There's a park not far from where I live. I can tell you how to find it. Let's meet there at one o'clock and I'll bring a picnic lunch."

They heard Abe's gruff voice. "Hey! The two of you quit talking and get some work done in there." Joe put his head down and began scrub-bing the pot he was working on. Emma hurried out the door with her order.

When Joe was growing up, he and his mom and dad went on a few picnics, but I was always left behind. The next day I got excited when I realized that Joe was taking me with him. My first picnic! The one thing that dampened my strings was the possibility that ants might crawl on me. I'd heard they always show up at picnics.

Emma spread out a blanket and laid out sand-wiches, apples, two Cokes and cookies.

"This is great, Emma. I suggest a walk and you show up with a four-course meal. Thanks. Very nice."

Emma lowered her head in a shy smile. Joe laid me on the blanket and picked up a sand-wich. As he ate, his eyes darted around, trying to find anything but Emma to focus on. Emma intently studied a nearby tree trunk. At work, roles were defined, but here, without Abe looking over their shoulders, they were free to talk about other things than pots and pans and someone's order. Each seemed unsure how to begin. Their awkwardness might have bothered me more if I hadn't been so busy watching for ants.

After Joe finished his sandwich, he said, "Would you like me to play something on my guitar?"

"Oh, yes! That would be wonderful."

Problem solved. Joe picked me up, and began to sing a song Mitch had taught him, a blues piece called, "Sweet Mama, Don't You Wait for Me." Emma's eyes twinkled as her head swayed with the music. When Joe finished, she threw her arms around his neck and said, "Joe, that was amazing! You are so talented."

I saw she had embarrassed herself with her exuberance, because she blushed and quickly released her arms. She effectively changed the subject by saying, "I notice one of the screws on the—hm-m. What do you call the things that poke out at the top?"

"Pegs."

"Yeah. I notice that all the screws on the pegs are silver but one, and that one is gold. Why is that?"

"One day when I was a kid, and my dad was gone, I went into the workshop and pretended to be making guitars. I took the screw out of that peg and accidentally dropped it. I couldn't find it."

I remembered that day well because I panicked. I felt like a tooth had been removed. What happened next turned out to be an improvement.

"I looked around and found a gold one to replace it."

Yes, I liked the gold screw and was worried Victor would want to remove it.

"My dad was cool about it. He let me keep the gold screw and didn't get mad." Joe looked wistful. "I don't remember my dad ever really getting mad at me." He cleared his throat and said, "I miss him."

That loosened things up and they began to talk. Joe told Emma how he ended up at Mayfield's Jazz Bar, and Emma talked about her life.

"My dad left when I was seven. I remember Mama crying a lot." She closed her eyes. Then looking up at Joe, she said, "My job at Mayfield's helps make ends meet, but it hasn't been easy." She smiled. "Since you've come to work, it's not any easier, but it's more fun."

We finished the afternoon on a high note as Joe took Emma's hand. Walking home, my top fret curved into a smile, reflecting the one I saw on Joe's face. When it came to emotions, we vibrated as one.

The bar at Mayfield's stayed open every night until 2 a.m., but dining and music stopped at ten. Sometimes Joe walked Emma home. One night, when we arrived at her door, he gave her a sweet gentle kiss. You might think I'd be jealous with the way Joe was giving attention to someone besides me, but I knew my place with Joe was secure. Bonded from birth, we were almost like twins. Besides, as I've said, when Joe was happy, so was I. On the way home, after leaving Emma at her doorstep, he began singing, and I think he would have skipped down the street if I had not been on his back.

One night when we left Mayfield's, I scanned the stage until I found J. T. I wanted to get a closer look at the man who could make his saxophone resonate with such a poignant musical language; the man who continually inspired the audience to clap and cheer as he made his saxophone speak—of love, of heartbreak, of sadness, of life. I saw him putting his instrument away. He was a big black man dressed in dark clothing. His curly hair was cropped close to his scalp. From looking at him, one could not predict his great talent. I longed to be able to actually watch him as he played.

Chapter 13

Then came the night that changed everything. As Joe, Emma, and I were leaving, J.T gave a holler.

"Hey Joe, can I talk to you a minute?"

Joe turned to Emma and said, "I'll see you tomorrow. Careful walking home."

He turned and we headed for the stage where band members were packing up their instruments.

J. T. stepped off the stage. "Joe, you've shown me you know a lot about music. I'm curious to hear you play your guitar. If you have a little time, why don't you come over to my place for some jamming and then I'll take you home."

"Sure," said Joe.

I could see Roy glaring Joe's way as he put his guitar in its case, but he said nothing. J. T., Joe, and I went out into the cool night to J. T's black Ford.

As he pulled away from the curb, J. T. said, "That's a beautiful guitar. Where did you get it?"

"My dad made it. He was a luthier—Victor Marcini."

"I've heard of him. Where does he live?"

"He died recently."

"Sorry to hear that."

"I miss him. He was a great dad." Joe paused, and then said, "He was my first guitar teacher."

There was silence in the car until we arrived at J. T.'s apartment. As we entered, J. T. flicked the lights on, and before us was a big front room decorated all in blue.

"Make yourself at home. Can I get you anything?"

"A glass of water, please. Thanks." Joe said.

While J. T. left to get water, Joe tuned me up. J. T. said I was beautiful. I was excited to show him just how beautiful, once Joe began to play me.

When J. T. returned, Joe nestled me under his arm and said, "I'll play a piece Mitch taught me."

"Who? Mitch Williams? You knew him?"

"Yes. I met him when he came to look at my dad's guitars. He wanted to buy this guitar, but my dad made it for me—finished it right when I was born. The two of us are inseparable."

"I understand. I love my sax the same way."

Joe continued. "Mitch asked me to play for him and he must have liked what he heard because he offered to give me lessons. My dad brought me into New Orleans once a week for lessons until Mitch moved."

Joe lifted me and began to play the song, "Dark Night on Bourbon Street." When he finished, J. T. clapped and said, "I don't think Mitch could have done it better. You want to play it again? I'll get my sax."

As we repeated the song, the musical dialogue between J. T.'s saxophone and me sent my spirits soaring, but then Joe, who had always played alone, now began improvising, our sounds dancing around the melody that J. T. was carrying on the saxophone. It was a first. I nearly came unglued. When the song ended, J. T. and Joe let loose with an excited cheer.

"Wow! That was over-the-top fantastic!" J. T. said. His eyes were on fire and his smile took up his whole face. This man loved music as much as we did. He sucked in air, almost like he'd forgotten to breathe, settled a little, and then asked, "Can you sing?"

"I like to think I can." Joe jumped into a blues number called, "I Can't Get Over You."

When he finished, J. T. shook his head. "Unbelievable! How would you like to join the J. T. Jazz Band? You won't get paid much, but playing guitar has got to be more rewarding than washing dishes."

Joe's eyes got big. "Really? There's nothing I'd like better." But then his face dropped. "Roy hates me. How is he going to react to a second guitar on stage, especially with me being the one playing it?"

"Roy is all bluff. It will be fine."

"And one more thing, J. T. Abe will have a fit. I'm his dishwasher."

"Hmm. You're right." His eyes looked up toward the left, thinking. "I have a great idea," he said with a smile. "My nephew needs a job. Let me talk to Abe. Maybe we can make everyone happy."

After J. T. dropped us off, Joe bounced up the steps. "Rose, we are beginning a new life." I was deliriously happy about our new direction, but after Joe turned out the lights and climbed into bed, I began thinking about Roy. An uncomfortable foreboding diminished my joy and kept me strung out half the night.

The next afternoon we showed up in the kitchen, as usual. Joe started washing the few dishes left from the night before. The band members began trickling in a little after five. A short while later I heard J. T. talking to Abe.

"Your dishwasher and I spent some time jamming last night at my apartment. He's good, Abe."

"Good for being just a kid, right?"

"No. It's more than that. Mitch Williams was his teacher."

"Well, I'm glad you think he is good on the guitar, but he is also good on the dishes." I heard a wariness in his voice. "I wouldn't want to lose him."

"Here's the thing, Abe. I want Joe to join our band, but before you get in a huff, I have a nephew who is looking for a job. I'm almost certain he will jump at the chance to be your dishwasher."

"I don't know. The kitchen is running smoothly right now. I hate to change things that are working."

"Joe is a surprise, Abe. Unique, refreshing, gifted. He'll bring in customers. At least give it a try."

"Let me think about it."

"I'll contact my nephew and have him come by to see you. His name is Marty."

The band began warming up. As I listened, I imagined Joe and me playing with them. I could almost hear my melodic, magical sounds mesmerizing the patrons. I imagined them cheering, "Do you hear that guitar? Amazing!" And "I can't believe my ears!" And "I've never heard anything like it!" I improvised similar scenes, daydreaming the rest of the evening away while Joe cleared tables and scrubbed dishes.

Marty came in the next afternoon. His voice was pleading as he spoke to Abe.

"I really need this job. If you hire me, you won't be sorry. You'll see."

Abe brought him into the kitchen and spoke to Joe. His voice was neutral, not unkind.

"I understand you want to join the band, Joe. This is Marty. Show him what you do, and we'll see."

Marty was shorter than Joe. He had a high forehead, topped with short curly hair. His crooked smile made me want to smile, too. He reminded me a little of J. T. I liked him immediately. As he and Joe were going over what Marty would be doing, Emma came through the door, stopped short, and with eyes wide, threw her hands into the air.

"Marty! What are you doing here?"

"You know Marty?" Joe asked.

"We went to school together."

"He's going to be the new dishwasher, or at least I hope he is." Joe said. "Last night after J. T. and I jammed together, he asked me to join the band."

Emma squealed. "Joe! That's wonderful!" She threw her arms around him and squeezed hard.

Marty eyed them and asked, "Is Emma your girlfriend or something?"

The blunt question rubbed my grain the wrong way, but Joe just smiled and said, "Maybe."

Emma immediately busied herself, but I could see a smile spread across her face.

At the grill, Joe introduced Marty to George and Rupert. "Besides our own jobs, we try to help out wherever needed, but I never get too close to George when he has the knife in his hand." George chuckled. As Joe and Marty walked back toward the sink, Joe said, "We don't have many dishes this time of day, so usually this is when I help Emma set up the tables."

Emma took Marty's arm. "Let me show you what we do out in the dining room." Marty followed her through the door, and when they returned, Joe showed him where clean dishes went and how to take out the garbage.

When Marty first arrived, I admit to being nervous. What if he was a flake? Joe's and my future was riding on his fitting in and being a good worker. As I watched, I began to relax, feeling hopeful that he would measure up to Abe's expectations.

With not much going on yet, Marty and Joe washed counters and straightened cupboards. I wondered how Marty was feeling about taking the job, but then, as so often happened, Joe picked up on my vibe. He asked Marty, "Well, what do you think? Are you up for mountains of dirty dishes every day?"

"For sure!" He pulled his hands out of the soapy water. "And my mom won't be complaining about my dirty fingernails." He lifted his fingers to show Joe. "Besides, I like working with you and Emma." He shook his head. "Oh yeah, that's right. I won't be working with you."

"I hope not." Joe laughed.

Toward the end of the evening, Abe came into the kitchen while Marty was clearing tables.

"What do you think, Emma? How is it working out with Marty? Does he pull his own load?" He gave her a piercing look as if he was trying to read her mind.

"Yes. He worked hard this afternoon and was open to suggestions. We'll be a good team."

I thought what Emma said was true, but I also knew she wanted to help Joe get into the band.

Her response was all that Abe needed. Marty would start as dishwasher the next day.

The following afternoon, dressed in clean pants and tee shirt, with me slung across his back, Joe hurried down the steps from our apartment so fast I didn't see how he kept from falling. Once outside, although I was on his back, he couldn't seem to help himself. He broke into a bouncy jog—his first day as a member of the band! I hoped the jarring wasn't loosening my pegs.

When we arrived at Mayfield's, J. T. was the only band member there.

"Welcome, Joe. I've told the others you'll be joining us. This is a list of the songs we'll be performing tonight. You can put your guitar on that stand that's sitting in the back."

Joe tuned my strings and sat me in place. He stood beside me while we looked over the list. A smile moved across his face from ear to ear. Yes, I was smiling, too, from left peg to right. We knew most of the songs. They were ones Mitch had taught us. And I was sure we could easily catch on to the others. I was so excited, I nearly jumped off the stand.

A short wiry man with bronze skin that appeared to glow, entered from the stage door.

"Joe. This is our drummer. He is from Puerto Rico. We call him Rico."

"Pleased to have you aboard, Joe." I liked his accent and wished he would say more.

Roy and another man entered.

"Joe, meet Roy—he plays guitar, and Sam—he's our piano player."

Roy, dressed in a tee shirt and khaki pants, ignored us. Sam, a man of medium height with black pants, long-sleeved shirt and red silky vest, tipped his straw fedora and shook Joe's hand. A cigarette hung from the side of his mouth, one eye closed to keep out the smoke.

J. T. spoke. "We'll start without Lou. He's running late."

I figured out Lou must be the bass player.

"Joe, why don't you stand in that spot over there by the piano." Band members positioned themselves with their instruments. I noticed no one had any written music in front of them.

"Let's begin our practice with the song Joe and I played together the other evening—'Dark Night on Bourbon Street,'" He paused. "Everyone ready? One, two...ah, one, two, three, four."

With drums and piano, the song sounded even better than when we played it at J. T.'s. Halfway through, J. T, stopped everyone and said, "Let's try Joe with a solo interlude here. Rico, go ahead with the drums."

Joe's fingers moved up and down my neck in rapid succession, doing things I didn't know we could do. J. T. brought the rest of the band back in and we ended the song.

"Holy Mackerel! That's the best the song has ever sounded," Sam said. "A mighty fine guitar you play there, Joe."

I glanced at Roy. His eyes were squinted, his mouth downturned. We started the next song, but part way through, he stopped playing and said, "Hold it!" Everyone stopped.

"What's going on, Roy?" asked J. T.

"This is nothing like what we usually do with this song. Joe is all over the place on his guitar, and it's not working for me. Things are getting all messed up." Roy paused. "I don't see two saxophones or two pianos on the stage. We don't need two guitars, either." Joe looked down at his shoes, like he was examining them for scuff marks.

"Calm down, Roy," said J. T. "Give it a little time. We can work it out. Joe is adding a new dimension that is making the band sound better."

"Don't sound better to me," said Roy.

We started the song again. This time Sam began doing some innovations on the piano. When we finished, everyone but Roy seemed elated.

"What you did on the piano that time worked well, Sam," said Rico. "I've never heard you do that version."

"I was inspired by what Joe did. What a gas! This is turning out to be a lot of fun!"

"It's not about fun," said Roy. "You think we're a bunch of kids playing around on some instruments? We're not! We're fixin' to perform—for people who are comin' to hear real music, not this doodlin' around."

The room went silent. I sensed Roy's feeling of inadequacy. He could play it straight, but as soon as musicians began getting creative, he wasn't sure how to fit in. I felt embarrassed for him. And for his guitar. I knew it didn't have conscious awareness, but I imagined that if it did, It would be feeling humiliated right now. Poor thing. But it would never do for me to scale down my rich sounds, or pretend I didn't know the riffs Joe was fingering, just so I wouldn't show up another guitar. No. My job was to shine. Clearly, Roy's guitar was never going to shine as long as Roy was the one playing it.

I heard the backstage door open. "Hey, I'm here. Sorry I'm late." Ah. The bass player. A big man, he had no trouble dragging the bass to its resting spot beside Rico. "What's going on? You're standing around like you've just seen a 'gator sidle across the room."

"We're working out some hitches, Lou," said J. T. With the silence broken, he turned to Roy. "We don't have time to spend arguing. Someone has to be in charge here, and it's me. We are going to continue with the two guitars."

"Well, no we aren't. Either Joe goes or I go." It was another long silence before J. T. spoke. With muscles taut, Joe was wound tighter than my high E string.

"I'm sorry to hear that, Roy, but my decision is final."

"I can't believe you are choosing this barely-out-of-diapers kid to replace me. I've been with you for a long time." Roy's face was red and distorted. He practically threw his poor guitar in its case. As he headed toward the stage door, he turned, pointed his finger directly at J. T. and said, "You'll be sorry for this." He stepped through the door and slammed it behind him.

Chapter 14

As soon as the door closed, I felt Joe's shoulders relax. Poor guy. It must have been hard to be the target of Roy's anger.

Talking had stopped at the bar. The four men sitting there were looking in our direction. Abe walked over to the stage, looked at J. T.and spoke gruffly. "What's the disturbance? We can't have this kind of thing going on in here."

"It's no longer a problem, Abe. Roy decided to quit."

Abe rubbed his chin, appeared to be thinking. "It's not my place to say, but Roy did bother me some. Maybe it's best. Go ahead and get on with your rehearsal."

With Roy out of the room, Joe's shoulders remained relaxed. As the rehearsal continued, the musicians responded to Joe's skill with smiles on their faces and a new focus to their playing. By the time the dinner crowd began to arrive, it no longer seemed we were rehearsing. We were in a groove. Anticipating each other's innovative moves, the music flowed in perfect sync. The rest of the world faded, and we were living the music.

I watched as Emma took people's orders. She was all business, but once in a while she flashed a smile Joe's way. We played slow, jazzy blues interspersed with be-bop that invited dancers to the floor. Because I was always hanging on the wall in the kitchen, I hadn't seen the dancing. At first only a few couples ventured onto the floor, but as the evening advanced, few remained seated. I wished I could dance, too. The rhythms were irresistible.

I was having such a good time, it took me a while to notice people were beginning to talk and point at Joe and me. Then I heard someone sitting near the stage say, "Get a load of the kid, Grant. He is unbelievable!" The man sitting next to him said, "Yeah, and where do you think he got that guitar? Holy moly!"

What they said tickled my fancy sides. It was my daydream come true! Encouraged by the praise, I raised the bar and put forth extraordinarily beautiful sounds for Grant and his friend, my new admirers. I began to hear others murmur and point. At the end of our next song, someone yelled, "Hey, J. T., who's your new band member?"

J. T.'s eyes twinkled. "This is Joe. What do you think?" People clapped and cheered. As we started the next song, people immediately jumped up to dance. The room was electric. I wanted Joe to pinch one of my strings so I could see if what was happening was real.

The evening ended with band members laughing and clapping each other on the back. The dinner crowd pushed back their chairs, stood and moved towards the door. Almost everyone had stayed through the whole evening. Grant and his friend came up to Joe and me.

"I'm Grant and this is my friend, Fred." They each shook Joe's hand. "You are a pistol on the guitar. Where'd you learn to play like that?"

"My dad was my first teacher, and then Mitch Williams."

"Ah, yes. Mitch. We all loved Mitch," said Grant. "I thought I recognized some of his riffs."

"That is a badass guitar you are playing there. You really make it sing," Fred added.

About that time, Abe called out, "Joe, that was killer diller music you were playing. I concede. You're a better guitar player than dishwasher."

Joe raised his voice above the din, "Thanks, Abe. I can't believe I'm playing with this dynamite band. It's the most fun I've ever had."

Tonight we had delivered a perfect pitch!

Emma finished clearing the last table, took off her apron, and the three of us left together. As Joe and Emma walked, Emma began humming the tune to one of the songs the band had played. Joe turned and looked at her, smiled, and began humming with her. They took each other's hand, began swinging their arms, and soon they were laughing. When we reached Emma's door, Joe bent and kissed her.

Emma showed a dimple as she said, "Your playing tonight lit Mayfield's Jazz Bar on fire. You were amazing! People loved you!"

Joe answered with another kiss, gave a shy smile and said, "Good night. See you tomorrow."

Instead of walking home, we floated—down the street, through the door of our apartment building, up the stairs, and into our room. Joe placed me on the stand and said, "Life is good, Rose. I couldn't do it without you."

All night I dreamed of people dancing, laughing, cheering—delighted to be in a place where so much good music was happening. Joe and me—a wonder team. Neither one good without the other. As the dawn brought in a new day, I felt a great hope for our future.

A couple of nights later when Joe was walking Emma home, Emma asked, "Joe, do you ever go to church?"

"No. It's not something our family ever did. How about you?"

"Sometimes my mom and I go to Saint Anna's Episcopal Church, which we walk to from our apartment."

"I'm not opposed to church,"said Joe. "I've just never thought much about it."

I listened carefully. I'd seen churches, but Joe had never taken me into one. I knew that the people who went, prayed and worshiped God. Is that why Emma went? To pray and worship God?

"I only bring it up because I think you would like the gospel music," said Emma. "Saint Anna's has a gospel choir that is fantastic. It's different music than what you play at Mayfield's, but I think you would like it."

"Tell me about it," said Joe.

"It's a mixed choir of men and women, singing in four-part harmony with bass singers, reaching notes so low you wouldn't believe it. The deep sound is like having a bass fiddle in the choir, only better."

"Hmm. That does sound like something I'd like."

"They sing with their whole hearts and souls, swaying and moving their arms. The church has a high ceiling. The acoustics make me think I can hear angels singing. It's really something."

"Yes, I'd like to go sometime," Joe stopped walking and looked at Emma, "but I have a problem."

"Oh? Like what?"

"I take Rose with me everywhere I go, but it seems strange that I would take her into the church with me."

"Rose?" Emma frowned. "Who's Rose?"

Joe laughed. "My guitar."

Emma laughed. "Your guitar has a name?"

"We've been together our whole lives. It seems natural that she would have a name."

"Well, that's a relief. I thought maybe you had a girlfriend on the sly."

He laughed. "I have you and I have Rose. That's enough for me." They began walking again.

"So what are your beliefs about God?" Joe asked.

Emma hesitated. She seemed to be thinking. "I'm not sure about anything, but I think there is a God. I don't know what he looks like or anything, but it seems impossible to think this world is just random with nothing beyond this life."

"Yes, I wonder about it, too," said Joe. "Sometimes at night, I lie in bed and think about my mama and papa. I don't know. Are they somewhere? Might they be watching over me?"

Joe and Emma's conversation got me thinking. I knew when Joe's mama and papa died there was no bringing them back. They were gone. I didn't give much thought to where they might have gone. Both Victor and Collette were good people. If heaven existed, they must be there. Then I wondered, *Would a guitar go to heaven? When Joe and I died, could I go with him?* Then it hit me. We will both age together, but when Joe is eighty, he'll have wrinkles and limp around. His body will have lots of aches and pains.

When I'm eighty, my sound will have improved. I remembered Victor telling his clients that a good guitar became more valuable as it aged, its sound mellowing, becoming richer. The realization hit hard. *When Joe is eighty, he will be on his way out, while, at the same time, I will be on the rise!* I felt sad. I wanted to be with Joe—always. If I could talk to him, I would beg, *Take me with you when you die!* But how would he even do that?

I realized I had gotten myself wound up way too tight. I needed to stop fretting about the future and go with the flow of the music Joe and I were making together now.

We arrived at Emma's door. "I don't know that we can figure any of this out, but it makes interesting conversation," said Joe.

"I haven't ever talked with anyone about these things. I have lots of questions. Thanks for being so open and easy to talk to."

Joe wrapped his arms around her, gave her a kiss and said good night. "See you tomorrow."

The next night at Mayfield's was even better than the two previous ones, if that was possible. Within a week, the dinner clientele had doubled. As people entered, I could see them talking and pointing—at Joe and me. I had heard the term, "word of mouth," but did not realize it was at least as effective as flashy, expensive advertising. But the following week the advertising appeared, too. Out front was a big poster that said, "Playing now with the J. T. Jazz Band, the amazing Joe Marcelli and his magic guitar."

Our fiery band continued to play each night to a packed audience. I saw a new girl waiting tables and realized Abe had hired her to help Emma. Yes, things had changed at Mayfield's Jazz Bar, one of the most noticeable being Abe. The usually gruff bartender now seemed like a jolly bear.

Then came a particular Friday night, with standing room only in the area of the bar. On stage we were into a jazzy song that had the dance floor hopping. When the song ended, the band took a break. Joe put me on the stand at the back of the stage and went to mingle with his admirers.

As I watched, a sixth string sense warned that something bad was going to happen. Within seconds of the feeling, Roy swaggered through the door. Behind him was a person who looked more like a gorilla than a man.

Roy pushed his way through until he was standing in the middle of the room, where he yelled, "What's up around here? Have you missed me?" His speech was slurred. Clearly, he was sauced. I watched the people near him avert their eyes and turn to talk to others close by.

Roy raised the pitch of his voice. "Where's that sissy guitar player you have now?" Fear amped me to a high-strung nervousness. My body shivered with a dark foreboding. What was going to happen here?

Roy spotted Joe and moved toward him. The gorilla followed close on his heels. Abe came from behind the bar and walked in their direction.

"We don't need any trouble, Roy," he said to a room that had become dead quiet.

Roy came up to Joe and gave him a shove. Abe moved quickly to Roy's side and tried to grab him. The gorilla turned and punched Abe in the jaw. Down he went. A couple of big men pushed their way into the knot of people surrounding Joe and Roy.

"Enough!" one of them yelled. He tried to grab Roy while the other man threw a punch at Roy's bodyguard. After that, it was pandemonium. People pushed each other, women screamed, others went down, unable to get back up. I was unable to do anything but watch. *Please don't let anything happen to Joe,* I thought.

I did not expect what happened next. Roy emerged from the uproar, and in spite of being blitzed, was able to jump onto the stage, grab me by the neck, and slip out the stage door. Had anyone noticed? I didn't think so.

Chapter 15

As Roy ran down the alley and into the street, my strings tightened until one broke. I was terrified!

A car was parked on the street by the alley. Roy laid me in the back and jumped into the driver's seat. In minutes, his bodyguard appeared at the driver's door, opened it and said,

"You're too bombed to drive. Move over."

"Okay, but we gotta get out of here fast, Barney."

"I know. Don't worry. I'll take care of it. C'mon! Move over."

"You know where we're going, right?"

"Yeah. Out of town as fast as we can—north."

Barney put the car in gear, revved up, and pulled away from the curb. At a stop sign he turned left, went two blocks and turned right.

"Whatcha doin', Barney? Yer not headin' North, yer goin' in circles."

"Don't blow a fuse, Roy. I'm ditchin' anyone who might be followin' us. I'll make a few more turns to confuse 'em." But Barney was the one who became confused. After ripping around this way and that, he said, "Dang! Where are we? I'm lost."

Roy lifted his drooping head. "I can't believe you, Barney. Get us out of this city. Now!"

"Well, help me. It's dark. I can't see anything."

"Like I said, meatball. Head north."

"Which way is north?"

"How am I s'posed to know? Find the North Star or somethin'."

I was hoping Barney would never find north, but as he drove up one street and down another, he eventually found the one that headed out of town. He eased the car onto a long straight road and hit the gas. The quick acceleration made me a little car sick—and a lot heartsick.

"See? No worries. No one coulda followed us."

"Humph!" Roy responded. Soon he was snoring.

I wished I was bombed like Roy. My strings would have a slurry, indistinct sound, but who would care? If I could pass out, I wouldn't have to think or feel for a while. I needed some relief from this downward glissando, this miserable turn my life had taken. I felt like someone was strangling me with one of my own strings.

Barney drove through the night, stopping once for gas. At dawn the sky turned pink and orange. He gave Roy a shove and said, "I gotta get some sleep. Yer turn to drive." He paused. "How ya feelin'?"

"Crummy. I'm about to up-chuck. Find us a motel."

Barney took one hand off the wheel and waved it in the air. "How we gonna get a motel?" He took a deep breath. "I'm out of dough. I bet you are, too."

"Cool down, will you? I have enough for a motel."

Barney fidgeted, his fingers tapping on the steering wheel. "Just how far north are we goin', Roy?" I could feel the worry in his voice. "This whole thing's makin' me nervous. What's yer plan?"

"We'll talk about it tomorrow. Right now I'm hammered. My headache is blinding me. I need aspirin and a bed."

Listening to Roy talk, I realized the price I would have to pay to get plastered. The next morning, I would ache all over and my strings would be fried. Would it be worth those few hours of forgetting? I was on the fence about it. If someone turned to me right now and said, "Hey, guitar. Looks like you could use a drink," I think I would have accepted. But no. I couldn't drink alcohol or anything else. Numbing in this way was not an option for a guitar. Terrible jabs of fear struck my hollow center.

A hollow center was part of my natural construction, so it wasn't something I was trying to get rid of. I just needed to go numb for a while. I sensed Roy had a hollow center, too, but his was not natural, not something he wanted. He probably got ripped so he wouldn't have to feel that emptiness. When he was drunk the hole was filled with alcohol. When he was sober, it was filled with anger. Even though I wanted to string him up, I felt bad that those seemed to be his only two options.

The motel room smelled like it hadn't been aired in weeks. Two single beds and a dresser filled the room. Off to the side, was a tiny bathroom that appeared to have no window. Roy laid me on the dresser, swallowed three aspirin, and kicked off his shoes. As the sun came up, Roy and Barney went down.

I laid there on the dresser all day, with my thoughts modulating, syncopating, and improvising. No matter how I looked at it, my joyful life was over. I would probably never see Joe again. The weight of the sadness nearly crushed my ribs.

In the late afternoon, Roy and Barney woke up. Roy stumbled out of bed, slumped into a chair, and pulled out a cigarette. The two men were smelling pretty ripe, but neither took advantage of the shower. Barney began pacing.

"We gotta talk, Roy. I helped you get the guitar and we're headed north, like you said, but we're outta money. How far north are we goin'?" His hands went out, palms up. "You got somethin' in mind?"

"You're whining, Barney. Stop flapping your lips. I've got a plan. Don't I always have a plan?" He sucked on the cigarette, then blew the smoke toward me. My sensitive rosewood sides shivered with disgust.

Barney got a quizzical look on his face. "I think I just felt something come from the guitar," he said. "Like it was upset, like it was somehow alive."

"What are you talking about? You're halluci-nating, Barney. Don't go nutso on me."

They both looked right at me. I sat still as stone.

"The tree this guitar was made from was alive." Roy pointed at me. "But the thing yer lookin' at sittin' there on the dresser? Just glued pieces of dead wood."

Roy didn't have a clue how alive I was. Glued pieces of dead wood—ha!

"Okay, okay," said Barney. "I'm probably still a bit sauced."

"Well, get your head clear if you wanna hear my plan."

"I'm fine. Whatcha got?"

"We're headed for Memphis because I know someone there who will gladly pay a big chunk of cash for this guitar."

"How do ya know that?"

"He used to give the kid lessons. It's a real peach of a guitar. I know he will want it."

He was going to try to sell me to Mitch Williams? My strings perked up. I felt like I was balancing on the edge of a clef as I leaned toward Roy, waiting to hear more. I remembered how, when each time one of Joe's lessons ended, Mitch picked me up and played. He always acted like he wanted me for his own. Dare I hope?

Roy lifted his chin up and rolled his eyes toward Barney. "You'll have to admit, my plan is brilliant."

"Yeah. I guess that's a pretty good one," said Barney. He pulled out his own cigarette and lit it. I wanted to scream, "Get me out of this stinking place! I'm going to smell like a burnt tree stump."

Roy smirked. "I put that show-off kid in his place. He's nothin' without his guitar. And now, what's even better is we're gonna get money for it."

Barney took a drag on his cigarette and said, "But we're not in Memphis. We can't get there on fumes."

"Relax, Barney. I have a plan. Remember? I always have a plan."

"Yeah? Like what?"

"I've got a little money left. We'll get coffee and food at that restaurant across the street. Then we're goin' to a drugstore to get first aid supplies."

"Say what?"

"You're gonna dress me up like a war veteran. I'll sit on the street with a donation can, and play the guitar. In no time, we'll have enough money to get on up the road."

"What're you gonna do about that broken string?"

"I got new ones in my guitar case."

What sleeze balls! I wanted to pitch a fit. I had no choice but to be a part of this charade. If there was a Heaven, then certainly there must be a Hell—the place these imposters were going. I'd heard that Hell was a hot fiery place. Would I go there because I was associated with them?

My worry called up the words of William Blake's poem "The Sick Rose." Joe read it to his dad in what seemed like another lifetime.

> *O rose thou art sick,*
> *The invisible worm,*
> *That flies in the night*
> *In the howling storm*
>
> *Has found out thy bed*
> *Of crimson joy*
> *And his dark secret of love*
> *Does thy life destroy.*

How did William Blake know? He had written this poem about me! "Worm" fit Roy perfectly. Roy, the worm, had found my bed of crimson joy and was now destroying my life. I didn't understand what Blake meant by "his dark secret of love," though. There was no secret love going on here. I wanted to take that part out, but my interpretation was probably too literal. I knew that the mark of any great poem was to have the words speak in a unique way with enough mystery that each reader could take from it her own understanding.

I gave a big sigh. Thinking of the poem had been a great diversion, but now back to the worm's plan. It made me so distraught, I thought I might break a second string, but then I'd have two inferior replacements instead of just the one. *Relax, Rose, relax.* If I had control over the situation, it would be easier. But I was a guitar. With no legs to take me away, I remained a captive. The strings across my heart felt like prison bars.

That night I laid and thought about Mitch. I was not created to be with the likes of Roy and Barney, a peacock among vultures. A small bit of hope seeped into my hollow belly, where the pain had been, and I fell into a peaceful sleep.

The next day with a splint on his leg and his head wrapped in gauze, Roy found a place in the city center to sit with the donation can, along with a sign that said, "War Veteran." He tuned my strings and began to play. Barney stood a ways off, watching.

Did I make myself sound horrible? I wanted to, but I couldn't. Tickle a child in the tummy and ask her not to laugh. Tickle my strings and ask me not to make beautiful sounds. Same thing. Not going to happen.

Roy played and sang some of the songs I'd heard him do when I hung on the kitchen wall in Mayfield's Bar. Although he was a mediocre singer, my rich sounds called to the people walking by. They smiled, complimented the music, and placed coins in the bucket. Every once in a while, Barney collected the money, probably hoping the emptiness of the bucket would encourage more donations. At the end of the day, Roy hobbled to the car, took me in the front seat with him, and climbed in. Barney got behind the wheel and as we left the city, Roy idly played with my strings as he talked.

"Can you believe it?" Roy started laughing. "We made a killing!"

"Yeah. We made a haul, all right," said Barney. "We have enough to get us to Memphis with money to spare."

Sick-o shysters. How could they stand to live with themselves?

"It's gonna be hard to give up the guitar. While I was playing it, I saw what a gem it is." He looked down at me. "Maybe I should keep it."

Oh good heavens! I'd have to kill myself.

Roy gave a snort. "I want the money more than I want the guitar. It will go for a good price."

The corner of Barney's mouth twitched. "Or maybe we could take the guitar and go on the road with you as a war veteran. After each time, we could spend the money, and when we ran out, we could move on to the next town and do it again."

Roy laughed. "Like in the story of the goose that laid the golden egg. The guitar is our goose."

I couldn't stand all this joking about filching money from unknowing donors. I popped a D string. D for demon, disgusting, derelict, double crosser, detestable, devious, and dirty two-timing dipwads. When the string broke, it whipped out and slapped Roy across the face.

"Ow! That hurt." Roy glared at me. "Forget anything good I've said about this guitar. I hate it."

I wanted to say, "Mend your ways, mister, or life will keep slapping you in the face."

Almost as if he realized what I was thinking, he frowned, and shoved me in the back.

"Now you have another broken string," said Barney.

"I'll take care of it later. I'm done with that goose for now."

All was quiet for a while, and then Roy's attitude brightened as he said, "I wonder how much money we have?" As his hand clinked the coins, they both started hooting and hollering. "Let's go have a drink to celebrate!"

At the next town, we pulled into a place near a bar.

"What're we gonna do with the guitar?" asked Barney.

"Just throw that old blanket over it." They left me like that, alone in the back seat with too much time on my strings. I was keyed up. What if the thing with Mitch didn't work out? So many things could go wrong. My thoughts were like a broken re-chord that played over and over. As each thought came circling past, I became more tense. I needed to find a way to untie the knots in my strings. I wondered about meditation. Why hadn't I thought of it before? I put my strings on a peaceful om vibration and fell into a deep sleep.

Chapter 16

Although I heard raucous voices, laughing and yelling, I was so far under, it took me a few seconds to remember where I was. Oh yeah, the back of the car. The noise jangled the nerves in my back and brought me fully awake. I longed for the peace that had been shattered.

As Roy and Barney climbed in and slammed their doors, the final bit of sweet silence was broken. Here I was again with these two bozos, but this time Roy was not the only one sauced. As Barney fumbled with the key, I realized how unsafe it was for him to drive. As he took a few bumpy jerks away from the curb, I hit my head on the door and almost broke my neck. My safety was in jeopardy!

"I don't know how far we can get down the road, but we need to put some distance between us and this town. We ruffled a few feathers."

I wanted to tell him he was ruffling my strings. He was too drunk to drive! The only way I could communicate this was through magic, but I was quite sure seeing pink elephants was the extent of Roy's and Barney's ability to notice any magic.

The car picked up speed. I could hear gravel spitting up from the wheels as the car swerved to the right.

"Criminy, Barney! Yer gonna kill us!"

Exactly! I was petrified wood. If we had an accident, they'd probably die and my precious body would become common kindling to stack in a woodpile.

"S'okay. I got things under control."

As we moved along, I saw that he did not have things under control. We were all over the road, the car swerving and straightening, swerving and straightening. Luckily, few other cars were on the highway this time of night. After nearly an hour, Barney turned down a dirt road and shut off the engine. My stricken strings slackened.

"I gotta sleep. I don't know how much farther it is, but I can't go anymore tonight." Barney grabbed the blanket that was covering me, laid it across his shoulders, put his head back, and fell asleep almost immediately. Roy's dull snore followed shortly.

The sun was well up before Roy and Barney stirred.

"What a miserable way to spend the night," said Roy. "I have a crick in my neck."

"My whole body has a crick in it," said Barney, "and I have a splitting headache. How far to Memphis?"

"I'd guess six hours," said Roy.

"Drivin' all day is gonna kill me."

"Don't be a baby, Barney." Roy looked out the window. "Let's get some fresh air and have a smoke. It'll perk us up."

I wondered why Roy and Barney would need fresh air if all they were going to do was stink it up with cigarette smoke, but better there than in here.

After smelling up the outdoors, they climbed back in, and we continued toward Memphis. Barney was revived only enough to whine and complain all the way to the outskirts of the city.

"Let's get a room and something to eat," Roy said. "Tomorrow we'll go searching for Mitch."

They left to get dinner, and my thoughts turned to Joe and Mitch. Who I really wanted to be with was Joe, but being with Mitch would be better than the company I was keeping now. I wondered ... was there a chance Mitch would return me to Joe? Probably not. Roy would have a story about how he got me, and I'm fairly certain Mitch would want me enough that he'd ignore anything that sounded fishy. Strong desire can dampen the faint cries of truth wanting to be heard.

Roy and Barney returned from dinner with cigarettes and a six-pack of beer. While they drank, smoked, and played cards, I laid on the dresser, thinking about Joe. I wondered what he was doing. Without me, had he gone back to being a dishwasher? I hoped Emma was staying by his side to comfort him. He was undoubtedly experiencing a great sadness. Never had he been without me. Across the miles, I knew he was aching for me like I was aching for him. I laid and thought about my dismal future without him.

In the morning, Roy said, "Let's get a shower. We don't want to offend the people we're going to meet."

"Memphis is a big city. How're we ever gonna find Mitch?"

117

"Don't be a dunce, Barney. Aren't I the guy who always has a plan? We go to the nightclubs and start asking questions. I promise you, this will be a piece of cake. Someone will know where Mitch is playing."

After their showers, Roy and Barney smelled better, but the motel room was a reeking, cluttered mess. My orderly tuning pegs were offended. Clearly, I was in another class than these two. They were uneducated, foul-mouthed street bums. I, on the other hand, could hold court with the queen. I wasn't a snob. A snob is someone who thinks she is better than others, but isn't. No, I wasn't a snob. I was the real thing.

Once again I was laid in the back seat of the car and off we went to find Mitch. I began to feel anxious as I realized how much my future depended on this exchange. I could feel butterflies in my cavity. They were so numerous they were colliding with each other.

"Take us into the city and drive around so we can get the lay of the streets," said Roy. "From doing that, I think we'll be able to see where most of the nightclubs are."

When we came into what appeared to be downtown, Barney began slowly driving up and down some of the busier streets. Roy jotted words onto a piece of paper. After some time had passed, he said, "It looks like our best bet is Beale Street.

If we don't have any luck there, Main Street and Vance Avenue also have nightclubs."

It was close to lunchtime when Barney said, "I'm hungry. Can we stop in this restaurant and get somethin' to eat?"

"Yeah. This looks like as good a place as any."

"You gonna leave the guitar in the back?"

"Maybe not. This is a big city. Who knows what kind of creep might try to break in?

I wanted to laugh out loud. Roy, the creep and thief, was worrying about being robbed by a creep. The thoughts swirling around in the dark place in Roy's mind were a reflection of himself.

"Grab it, will you, Barney?"

It? It? All they ever called me was "It." I'd had about enough. I was "her," not "it." My thin-skinned body was all bent out of shape. Joe would never call me "it." To him, I was Rose, a valued and beautiful guitar. True, Roy did value me—for the money he could get.

Then I thought of Mitch. He wasn't Joe, but he would treasure me. To him, I would not be an "it." The thought eased me out of my funk.

When we entered the restaurant, Roy and Barney chose a rectangular table in view of a large circular bar. The way Roy laid me across the end of the table felt awkward, but there seemed to be no other option.

While they were eating, a broad-shouldered man with a red beard and glasses, who looked to be thirty-something, walked up, inspected me and said, "I've never seen a guitar like that. Where'd you get it?"

"Bug off," Roy said.

The man stepped back like he'd been slapped. "You need to be careful how you talk to people, mister," he said. "You could get yourself in big trouble."

"Yeah, well, you can get yourself in big trouble if you don't bug off," said Roy.

The man's eyes darted fire, but he left and sat at a table nearby. Roy and Barney finished eating.

"Why don't you pay the bill?" said Roy. "I'm going to the can." He left and Barney looked around for a waitress.

The bartender yelled, "You can pay your bill here." I watched Barney do his gorilla walk to the bar.

A hand went around my neck. Smoothly but rapidly, Red Beard walked with me out the front door and past the restaurant's windows, then broke into a flat-out run.

What? I was being stolen again? Put a big repeat sign on my life. It was nice to know I was in such high demand, but this was way too much excitement. Unlike Roy, this guy didn't seem to have a plan. I felt he grabbed me on impulse, not liking to be talked to as if he were a nobody—an "it."

He jerked me back and forth as he ran, sometimes bumping me against his leg. Youch! We weren't far from the restaurant when I heard Barney yelling from behind. "Thief! Thief! Stop that man. He has my guitar!"

Your guitar? This was unbelievable! A thief chasing a thief. If I wasn't so traumatized, I would have busted a string laughing.

Barney was running, closing the gap, his bowed legs surprisingly speedy. Without me in hand, Red Beard could have probably gotten away, but I broke his stride.

From further back I could hear Roy. " Keep going, Barney! Yer catchin' 'im!" When Barney was within a few feet of my captor, Roy yelled, "Be careful with the guitar." Roy wanted me all in one piece, maybe the only thing in which we were of one a-chord.

Barney was upon us. He grabbed my sides with both hands, pulling. The running stopped. Red Beard began tugging, hard. *Yikes! Careful with my neck!* It didn't take long for Roy to catch up. With Barney holding onto my sides and Red Beard holding onto my neck, Roy slugged Red Beard in the nose. With blood running down his face, Red Beard still hung on. *My neck! Careful, careful! And watch the blood. Ew! Please! I can't abide that messy red stuff dripping on me!*

By now we had attracted a small crowd, which in turn, attracted a policeman who came running.

"Hold it!" he yelled. He pushed Roy away from Red Beard and said forcefully, "Hand me the guitar." Red Beard wiped his nose on his shirt sleeve and held out the guitar for the policeman.

Roy said, "It's our guitar, officer."

Red Beard countered, "They're lying. It's mine."

The officer said, "Well, for sure, one of you is lying."

Both are lying! It niggled at me that I couldn't rag on them. But being mute, I could only watch in frustration.

Roy said, "I can prove it's ours. Hide the guitar so this man can't see it, and ask him what is unusual about one of its pegs." I've always thought Roy wasn't playing with a full set of strings, but his question was clever. I would grant him that.

The policeman asked the man, "What is your name?"

"Harry," he said.

"Well Harry, can you answer the question?" Harry looked like he was thinking, but he didn't say anything. The seconds ticked by.

Finally, Roy said, "I'll tell you, Officer. One of its pegs has a gold screw. All the rest are silver." After taking a look, the officer handed Roy the guitar.

"Come with me, Harry," he said.

Roy and Barney turned and walked toward the car. "We've been put through the wringer, Barney. What happened? How did Harry get the guitar?"

"I left the table to pay the tab."

"You meatball! What were you thinking, leaving the guitar laying on the table like that?" Roy threw his hands up in the air. "Stupid, stupid, stupid!"

Barney didn't say a word, just walked with his head down.

About halfway back to the car, Roy let out a yelp. "Get a load of this!"

Barney stopped and gaped at the flyer on the lamppost. Big letters read, "MITCH WILLIAMS COMBO, playing at the Blue Heaven Nightclub on Beale Street, Tuesday through Saturday, 8 p.m. to midnight."

Chapter 17

"Well, what do you know about that?" said Roy. "Our search has come to an end."

Barney put his hands in his pockets, looked down and kicked a beer can. "That's all well and good, but the music starts at eight. What are we going to do for six hours?"

"Don't knock me over with your excitement, Barney." Roy turned and looked at him. "And quit your whinin'. Try your hand at comin' up with a plan."

"Yeah, well, I have a plan—we go to a motel so I can sleep."

"Lousy idea. We're runnin' outta dough."

They walked toward the car.

Barney began to say something.

"Shut up. I'm thinking," Roy barked.

They reached the car and Roy said, "Let's get some beer and go to a park where we can smoke and hang out. You can sleep on a bench."

After stopping for beer and cigarettes, Barney drove us around until he found a small park. Down at one end a mother was watching her two kids play on the slide.

"This looks good, Barney. Park the car and grab the beer. I'll get the guitar."

Roy leaned me against a tree. As he and Barney drank beer, they talked.

"I can still see that dufus goin' out the door with the guitar and me chasin' 'im." said Barney. "It's a good thing I'm fast."

"What you mean is it's a good thing I didn't strangle you for leavin' the guitar with no one watchin' it."

"But I made up for it. I got the guitar."

"No." said Roy, "I got the guitar—with my quick thinking." Roy took a big swig of beer. " I'm beginnin' to think this guitar is creating too many problems. Even though it's beautiful, the sooner we're rid of it, the better."

Could I help it if I created problems? I was not a wallflower. My beauty created a swirl of energy around me that caused people to sit up and take notice. Wherever I was, things happened.

Barney yawned and laid down on the grass.

Roy put a new D string on me and began strumming while humming a tune he had sung at Mayfield's Bar. The last time I heard it, Joe and I were together, happy, anticipating a great future. I was overwhelmed with nostalgia. The events of the past day had kept me from thinking about him. A few chords and a little humming brought me right back to Mayfield's Bar.

As I slowly emerged from my musings, I noticed the marvelous sounds coming from my strings—sounds enriched as they resonated with the wood and amplified through my hollow body. I became enthralled with myself and the nostalgia eased.

Toward evening, Barney sat up and said, "I'm hungry. Let's get somethin' to eat."

"You're always hungry," Roy said. He lifted his face upward and closed his eyes. "Hold on. Let me think." He opened his eyes and gave a smug smile. "Thinking pays off, Barney. You should try it sometime."

Barney's face showed no sign that he had heard Roy's negative comment.

Using my strap, Roy hoisted me onto his back as he and Barney walked to the car.

"Here's the plan. We eat at the Blue Heaven Nightclub where Mitch is playing. We scope out the place and decide on how to hit him up."

"Fine with me," said Barney.

Because of the time spent in the morning learning the city, Barney had no trouble finding the nightclub. It was seven o'clock when we entered, an hour before Mitch and his band would begin. I tried to stay composed, but I was nervous. Would Mitch recognize me?

The stage was located at the back of the room, the bar and kitchen off to the right. A waitress seated Roy and Barney at a small table about halfway between the bar and stage. Roy leaned me against a nearby chair. While the two were looking at a menu, a man dressed in black sat down near our table. He also began looking at a menu. I was admiring his hair, combed in a ducktail, when he turned to look at Roy and Barney. He spotted me standing nearby and bent down to get a better look.

"Your guitar is unusual." He stood and came closer. "I could swear I've seen it before." He looked up at Roy. "Where did you get it?"

"From a friend," said Roy.

This response was a soft version of the "Buzz off!" he'd used with the guy at lunch. I guessed he was trying to stay low-key to keep the interaction from escalating into something that would ruin his chance to talk to Mitch.

"You look familiar, too," said the man. He thought for a moment. "I know! You played with the J. T. Jazz Band at Mayfield's Bar in New Orleans. I live here now, but I go back and forth between here and there on business. I heard you play a few times over the past six months."

"Well, I'm glad I made some kind of impression," said Roy.

"But you had a different guitar," the man said.

"You seem to know a lot about guitars. Do you play?" Roy spoke in a high pitched voice. I could feel his nervousness quivering in his throat.

"Yes, but nothing like you or Mitch. I have followed Mitch for years. He and I moved to Memphis about the same time." He paused a moment. "Recently, I spent some time in New Orleans. The J. T. Jazz Band took on a young kid who was amazing. I wasn't there the night his guitar was stolen, but the following night, it was all anyone could talk about."

Barney spoke up. "Yeah, the guys who stole it should be strung up."

The man looked questionly at Barney. "The guys who stole it? Do you know something?"

Very soon this guy was going to put two and two together. I didn't know if I should be happy or scared.

Roy stood abruptly. "Barney, I just realized I don't have my wallet. I must have left it at the house." He turned to the man. "Excuse us. We have to go."

Roy grabbed me and we boogied out the door.

Roy's face contorted. "You idiot, Barney. 'The guys who stole it?' You might just as well have taken a finger and pointed it at us."

Barney put his head down, didn't say anything.

"From now on, keep your trap shut," Roy said. "When I talk to Mitch, don't say a word."

"Okay, okay," said Barney.

Roy took a deep breath. "That was close. This guy who heard me play In New Orleans comes and sits down right by us. What are the chances?"

I was sorry I didn't get to hear the man say more. What had Joe done after I was stolen? Maybe this man knew something. I still hadn't adjusted to the abrupt separation. I knew everything about Joe and then—nothing. What of Emma? Was she with Joe? Had Joe bought another guitar?

"What do we do now?" asked Barney.

"Let's see if we can find a restaurant near here so we can talk."

As Barney was driving, Roy said, "I see a sandwich shop up ahead. Stop in there."

"Fine. Anything. I'm starving."

With sandwiches in front of them, Roy began thinking things through. "We can't go back in there tonight. That man who knew me might not stay until the end, but we can't take the chance."

"Then we have ourselves a problem."

Roy spoke irritably. "Of course we have ourselves a problem. What do you think I'm saying?"

Barney didn't respond. Roy was always grumpy with Barney, but it didn't seem to affect Barney much. He was a half-step off from a full range of notes, and maybe not too sharp, but certainly his feelings must get hurt. Maybe the two of them had a deeper bond that helped Barney put up with Roy's short temper. Or more likely, Roy kept company with Barney so he could feel smart, and Barney hung around because he had little confidence in his own abilities.

Roy munched on his sandwich awhile, then quickly lifted his head. "Here's what we do. We catch Mitch when he's leaving the nightclub. It's the only way."

"Mitch'll think we're robbing him."

"No. We'll tell him we want his autograph. And then while he's giving it to us, I'll show 'im the guitar."

I began to squirm with uneasiness—the same worry. My future depended upon this exchange. I had no certainty Roy and Barney could pull it off.

Barney spoke. "Okay, but now we have to wait again. I hate waiting."

"You'll make it. We'll return to the park and sleep in the car until eleven thirty. That way we'll be back at the nightclub before Mitch comes out at midnight."

At eleven thirty, we were once again parked on Beale Street near The Blue Heaven Nightclub. A few people were trickling out.

"The streetlamp helps, but how will you know which one is Mitch?" asked Barney.

"Think, Barney. He'll be carrying a guitar." Roy jumped out of the car, grabbed me and said. "C'mon. Let's go hang out at the door."

A little after midnight, I could hear men talking together as they came out the door. Two of them were sharing the weight of a large black case that must have held a bass fiddle.

"Where's Mitch?" whispered Barney.

"Shush!" said Roy.

About that time out came a man carrying a guitar. He was talking to the man next to him. He was older, a little heavier, but it was Mitch, for sure. I recognized his voice.

Roy spoke in an upbeat, excited voice. "You were great tonight, Mitch! Can we have your autograph?"

"Sure," said Mitch. He pulled out a pen and began scribbling his signature on a notebook Roy held up. Then he picked up his guitar and turned to leave.

"Wait!" said Roy. "I have something to show you." Roy pulled me off his shoulder.

"Sorry. Not this time. We're tired. HaveA a good night."

"All I'm asking is for a minute of your time," said Roy.

Mitch looked back over his shoulder. "Are you deaf? No."

"Please. You won't be sorry," whined Roy.

Mitch faced Roy. "The bouncer is just inside the door. Leave me alone or—" Mitch was looking straight at me now. "That guitar. Where did you get it?"

"A guy named Joe sold it to me," said Roy.

I just about came unstrung with Roy's bald-face lie, but at the same time, I was hanging on every word, my strings quivering with the uncertainty of what would happen next. I had no backbone for this kind of suspense.

Mitch glared at Roy. "Joe. I know Joe. He would never have parted with that guitar. No way would he sell it. So tell me again, how did you get that guitar?"

Roy didn't miss a beat. "Really. Joe was down and out. He needed the money. I was going to keep the guitar for myself, but I've changed my mind. I thought you might like first stab at it."

"How did you know I knew Joe?"

"I heard you gave him lessons when he was younger. I'm up visiting my aunt and saw the flyer about your combo."

"Does Joe's dad know Joe sold his guitar?"

"Joe's dad is dead," said Roy. The impact of that information created a few seconds of silence.

Roy backed away. "I'm sorry I bothered you. I have a couple of other people interested in the guitar. We'll be on our way."

"Hold on," said Mitch. He put his head down. He seemed to be thinking. Lifting it again, he said, "Yes, I am interested in buying it. How much?"

"Five hundred dollars."

"No dice. The price is way too high. I'm not paying that."

"This is one of a kind. Victor was a famous guitar maker, as you know. The price of all Victor's guitars is going up now that he's dead."

The shorter of the two men carrying the bass fiddle was listening, balancing the instrument on the sidewalk. The taller man, who was also listening, said, "Okay Ace, let's get this into the back of the car and you can go."

Mitch said to Roy, "I'll give you three fifty."

Barney piped up. "Boy, that's great! What do you think, Roy?"

"Excuse us a minute. We want to talk about your offer," Roy said. We moved out of hearing distance.

"You bozo!" said Roy. "Didn't I tell you to keep your trap shut?" He was whispering, but spitting each word out with exaggerated emphasis.

"I was just tryin' to help," Barney whispered.

"You're not the one doing the negotiating. We can get more than three fifty." Roy shook his head. "You can help by sitting in the car."

Barney turned and walked away. Roy and I joined Mitch.

"I've decided four hundred is as low as I'll go."

"Wait a minute. Your friend agreed to three fifty," said Mitch.

"The guitar belongs to me, not to Barney. My offer is final."

"I see," said Mitch. He reached out his hands. "Let me check it for damage. I can't believe you're carrying it around without a case."

"Joe didn't have a case. He always used the strap to carry it on his back."

The last time Joe and I saw Mitch, I remember him telling Joe to take good care of me. I wanted Mitch to know Joe wasn't irresponsible. If only I could tell him, "Don't get the wrong idea. Joe had a case for me, but when we made our escape from a crazy drunk, it got left behind."

After inspecting me, Mitch said, "Okay, I'll pay four hundred. Meet me here just before eight tomorrow night. I'll bring the money and a case."

Was this really going to happen? Would my life with Roy and Barney soon be water under the bridge? Although feeling high strung and excited, I was still cautious, not counting my chickens before they hatched. Until the actual exchange took place, I would be on edge.

Even so, I couldn't help but think about how it would be with Mitch—how carefully he would lay me into the case, like a father laying his child gently into her cradle. I ached for that tenderness, like what I used to get from Joe. Waiting until tomorrow night seemed like an eternity.

"I'm going to push off now, Mitch," said the man who had directed Ace to put the bass in the car. "See you tomorrow night—maybe with a new guitar." He smiled. "It's a beauty."

"Yeah, Bye, Sal. Good job tonight. The bass sounded particularly good on that last number."

Mitch handed me back to Roy, who said, "We'll meet you here just before eight tomorrow night then." With that we were back in the car and on our way to a motel.

♪ Chapter 18

That night as I lay on the dresser, I pictured my life as a symphony. The first movement, a sonata in allegro, began with Joe's and my birth. The melodies were cheerful and lively, up until Joe began learning to play me, at which time the composition became loud and forceful. The sonata eased into expressive harmonies as Joe's playing improved. With Collette's death and then Victor's, the theme changed, with many unresolved chords that created an almost unbearable tension, which continued until Joe and I arrived in New Orleans, where the music resolved into a sweet melody. That period was interspersed with musical phrases that were quiet and lyrical, along with the same cheerful and lively tempo heard at the beginning.

The second movement, andante, began with a range of tempo, first the turbulence and surprise of Roy's and Barney's theft, turning to a slow, sad minor key, reflecting my heartbreak, as the three of us left to go north. Once we reached Memphis, the movement gained momentum. My emotions went up and down the minor scales, as if I were riding a musical roller coaster.

What next? Would my life be conducted into a third movement Scherzo, a joyful dance, or would I continue with the crashing and banging of cymbals, the horns blowing loudly, the violins dragging out the minor notes of a continuing second movement?

I was glad I wouldn't be seeing Roy and Barney anymore, but I didn't know what to expect from Mitch. I had been hanging onto the faint hope he might try to return me to Joe, but when I heard him make the deal, I realized he would now consider me his. As happy as I was to belong to him, he wasn't Joe. I would be one of his beloved guitars, but I wouldn't be Rose, the apple of his eye.

I experienced confusion of emotions: relief that I would be getting away from Roy and Barney; excitement with anticipation of beginning a new life with Mitch; sadness that Mitch wasn't Joe; and nervousness about my uncertain future. I over-thought things until my head hurt. Throughout the long night, I alternated between being amped up about my new life and fretting about the uncertainty of it.

As the exchange took place the following evening, I didn't feel the slightest remorse. Roy and Barney took the money and disappeared. Good riddance!

Mitch opened the case he brought and laid me gently into it, just as I imagined he would. It was lined with plush velvet. I felt a contented sigh escape through my heart as I nestled in. For the first time since I was snatched away from Joe, I felt safe.

Mitch, speaking to no one in particular, said, "Oh good. I see the case fits perfectly." He closed it, putting me into complete darkness. As before, when enclosed in a case, I had a claustrophobic panic moment. I focused on the comfort of the velvety interior and silently hummed the ABC song until I felt better.

By the balanced way he walked, I could tell that along with me, Mitch was carrying another guitar. I knew we were in the nightclub when I heard glasses clinking and people talking. A few people acknowledged Mitch as he moved toward what I assumed was the stage.

"Hi, Sal. The guitar is mine," Mitch said.

"Cool! I was hoping you'd buy it. What a beauty."

This was the same voice I heard last night—the bass player. While Mitch and Sal continued to talk, I listened to muted voices, along with the shuffling of feet and scraping of chairs coming from the nightclub floor.

Someone else entered the stage area. "The place is packed tonight," he said.

Mitch said, "Yeah, let's get ready to play. Ace, can you get Sal's bass set up?"

Who was Ace? I thought back to last night. It was Ace who helped Sal carry the bass fiddle to the car. He must be a stagehand.

"Good evening, friends," Mitch's voice projected above the talking. "Nice to see everyone. We have a great night ahead of us. Please step onto the dance floor when the music tells you it is time to move."

The night began with a jazz number. A piano and saxophone added to the guitar and bass to create music I wanted to be a part of, either by dancing or by adding my own resonant strains, but since guitars don't dance, and I couldn't play myself, I settled for feeling the rhythms course through my stringed veins as I laid in the case. I experienced the excitement in the room as I heard swishing skirts and tapping, shuffling feet.

At the break, Mitch opened my case, took me out and tuned me.

"What do you have there?" said a tall dark-skinned man, getting up from the piano.

"This is a guitar I just bought. It used to belong to a student of mine who lived in New Orleans." He tightened my E string a bit more and then hit a chord.

"Beautiful tone! That is a swell piece of work." said the piano player. "Are you going to use it tonight?"

"I thought I would."

"Cool!"

My debut at the Blue Heaven Nightclub was about to begin! I was giddy.

Mitch fingered my strings quietly until the break was over. "Are we ready?" he asked, looking around at the band members. "Let's get groovin'."

The rest of the evening was a blur. I thought the nightclub might explode from the fiery excitement in the room—people drinking, dancing, laughing and singing. Mitch's fingers were all over the place, stroking, tapping and plucking my strings with supreme agility and finesse.

At midnight a surprising number of people were still hanging around, some a little worse for wear. A few were so buzzed I wondered if they could make it through the door and into their cars.

Mitch was getting ready to put me in the case when I saw the same man that talked to Roy and Barney yesterday—the one who had recognized me. He purposefully worked his way toward the stage,

"Fantastic performance tonight, Mitch. I'm Jeff."

"Yes, I've seen you many times in my audiences. Nice to meet you."

"You brought the house down with that guitar. I'm surprised to see you with it, though. Just yesterday I talked with two men here at the nightclub who had it with them." He cleared his throat, seeming nervous. "It's not a guitar I'd forget. I saw it in New Orleans awhile back."

"Where?"

"At Mayfield's Jazz Bar. When I talked with the two men, I couldn't quite place it, but now I'm sure it belonged to the new kid the J. T. Jazz Band took on."

"What was the new kid's name?" Mitch asked.

"Joe. Like I told the two men, I wasn't there the night it was stolen, but I came the next night, and the bar was buzzing with the news."

"Stolen? His guitar was stolen?"

"Yeah. The two men left here immediately after I mentioned the theft."

"So you weren't there the night the guitar was stolen?"

"No, but like I said, I came the following night. Joe wasn't there, but I overheard one of the waitresses talking. She seemed to know him well. She said that sometime in the future he might buy another guitar, but right now he was mourning the loss of his best friend."

I went into a spin. We had each lost our best friend. Joe would buy another guitar, but it wouldn't be Rose. I had a different owner now, but he wasn't Joe. I thought my heart would break.

"I appreciate the information, jeff. Have a good night."

I wasn't sure what Mitch would do with this information. My imagination began playing with the thought of being returned to Joe.

In his small house, Mitch sat me on a stand near the couch. Throughout the following days, he often pulled me into his arms and played. He would close his eyes, and with his long graceful fingers, fill the room with a vibration that brought me joy. In the following evenings at the nightclub, I noticed new improvisations he included that he had created during the day as we spent our time together.

A shapely dark-haired woman named Bella came over most days around noon, which was about the time Mitch woke up. She put lunch together for them and they caught up on what

they'd been doing. On Sundays and Mondays—
the two days Mitch didn't work—the two of them
left me to go out for dinner or a movie.

One afternoon, when they were sitting together on the couch, Mitch cleared his throat, shifted
uncomfortably and spoke.

"Bella, I need to get something off my chest
that's been bothering me. Maybe if I tell you, I can
figure out what to do."

"Of course."

"You know how much I love this guitar, right?"

Bella nodded.

"Well, it has a history."

"I know you bought it from a couple of guys a
while back."

"Yes, but there is more to the story. Five years
ago, when I was living in New Orleans, I gave
guitar lessons to a twelve-year-old boy, son of Victor Marcini, a famous guitar-maker. Joe was the
kid's name."

"I've never known you to give lessons. What
was different this time?"

"I visited Victor's workshop one day and met
the boy. He played for me on a guitar his father
made for him. I was so impressed, I wanted to
take him further with his playing. Joe told me
he and the guitar came into the world about the
same time and that they were inseparable."

"That is sweet. How long did you give him lessons?"

"For two years. He made remarkable progress. We were to the point where we jammed side by side as equals. The lessons ended when I moved here."

"That's a touching story."

"This guitar? It is the one I'm telling you about. The two men sold me Joe's guitar."

"What are you saying? You said Joe wouldn't have parted with it."

"The two men told me Joe's dad died and that Joe needed the money."

"How sad."

"What's really sad is that a man came up to me at the club awhile back and told me Joe's guitar was stolen."

"Stolen? No!"

"Without knowing it, I bought a stolen guitar from a couple of thieves."

Bella put her hands to her face. "Oh, Mitch!"

"You realize my dilemma, don't you?" Mitch stood up and paced the room while Bella looked at him intently. "I love this guitar," he said. "I paid a lot of money for it, and I don't know where the men are that sold it to me. I suppose I could reason that the guitar is mine, but it doesn't feel right to keep it."

My thoughts exactly! Take me back to Joe! Please!

"I understand your torment, Mitch. I see no easy solution. If you return the guitar, you are out the money and you lose a guitar you love. If you keep it, you feel bad."

"I know. I'm going to sit with the problem for a few days before I make a decision. Meanwhile, I will delight in playing this exceptional instrument for as long as I decide to keep it. I've never seen a guitar that, besides being beautifully crafted, has the resonance and tone of this one. I understand why Joe never wanted to part with it."

This got me thinking. If I could dumb down my wonderful resonance and tone, possibly Mitch would tire of me, and it would be easier for him to let me go. I had an Achilles peg, though. When someone of Mitch's talent began strumming me, I was like a cat being stroked. I couldn't help but purr.

Although Mitch was stuck with this dilemma, I was not on the fence about it. There was only one thing to be done, which, of course, was the right thing—give me back to Joe. By inadvertently taking ownership of me, Mitch had a personal stake in what was to be done, but I had a personal stake, too—called my life!

For Mitch, being out the four hundred dollars was a big deal in itself, but to complicate things, he didn't want to part with me. How could I appeal to Mitch's altruistic side? He was a good person, but he had a big weakness—me. Is this how a girl feels when loved by two men? Unlike a girl, I had no control. I couldn't choose and then walk away, leaving one of the suitors behind. I had no trouble choosing, but beyond that, I had to wait and hope.

I could tell I had not yet left the second movement of the symphony. I was feeling a long, drawn-out appoggiatura, a poignant tension that creates emotional yearning before the notes ease into the relief of the sweet principal chord. I ached for that resolution.

Attempting to dampen this string of thought, I settled into my new routine, appreciating that I no longer spent nights in the car, a hotel or the city park. I looked forward to the evenings at the Blue Heaven Nightclub with Mitch. Traditionally, he brought in a good crowd, but as each night passed, I saw more and more people out on the floor doing the swing and the boogie woogie. They were laughing as they be-bopped and jived the night away. Mitch's fingers talked to my strings and my strings responded with joy and enthusiasm. The other band members came alive, too, just like at Mayfield's Bar, but this time there was no Roy to break the rhythm.

One evening before the band began to play, a big man in a suit spoke to Mitch. "I didn't think it possible to get any more tables or chairs into this place, but we've managed. Since you began playing your new guitar our clientele has nearly doubled." He shook his head. "It's hard to believe. You've always been a great musician, but when you picked up that guitar, something magical happened. I'm going to start calling you the Pied Piper."

Mitch laughed. "I know. This guitar is something, isn't it? I've always felt it was unusual."

"You make it sound like you've had the guitar for a long time."

"Well, no. But I knew the luthier who made it and the boy who played it. I gave him lessons a number of years ago." Mitch looked down at me. "The guitar just recently fell into my hands."

I lapped up every word of the conversation. Magic? The manager hit the peg on the head. I loved when others noticed. Even though the manager and Mitch had no idea just how magical, my unusualness could not be denied. The only source of irritation in that little exchange was "fell into my hands." I wanted to say, "Placed in your hands by thieves, Mitch."

♪ Chapter 19

One night, when everyone was packing up, Mitch looked at equipment still lying around and said, "What's going on here, Ace? You can't seem to move your feet." He stopped and looked at him. "Are you alright?"

"Yeah, I'm okay. I'll get going here."

"Good, because I'd like to get out of here some-time tonight."

I looked at Ace more closely. Medium height, with slumped shoulders, he wore a long-sleeved shirt that looked slept in, and pants that hung down over his shoes. I wondered when he'd last had a haircut. Although he said he was okay, he wasn't acting it. He began to put Sal's bass in its case, but before he'd finished, he wandered over and began moving a microphone. His face was screwed up like he was thinking about something that had nothing to do with putting instruments away. What was up with him? Curiosity was just about to kill the catgut strings. Wanting to know more, I decided to pay closer attention to this dis-tracted, strange man.

Although the band finished playing at mid-night, the bar stayed open until two. Often Mitch stayed to visit with friends. On these nights, adding to Ace's job of breaking down and putting away the music equipment, Mitch asked him to put me in the trunk of the car.

It bothered me that I couldn't remain to take in the fun and conversation. But because I couldn't, I laid in the trunk and pretended I was still inside the nightclub. I imagined Mitch setting me on a bar stool and asking me what I wanted to drink.

"I'm a teetotaler," I would say.

"That's okay," he'd say. "Let me introduce you to my friends."

After the introductions, the conversation would center around me, of course—how incredibly beautiful I was in construction, how magical my sound. I loved passing the time this way, play-acting make-believe scenarios.

As the next month went by, unbelievably, I rarely thought of Joe. I was in my realm, doing what I loved, with a master guitarist who cared about me. For now, things couldn't be better, knock on wood. People came to hear our music and to admire me. I was living in the beat of the moment, loving what I was doing, rather than moaning about the life I couldn't have. Releasing myself from my yearning and misery freed me to give all my energy to the music we were playing. I was high, alive with the sounds coursing through my body, the effect reflected from the admiring faces of the people.

Mitch talked a few more times with Bella about his moral dilemma on whether to keep me or try to find Joe. The fact that he continued to talk about it meant he hadn't forgotten. Putting off making a decision was probably troubling for him, but I think his time with me was sweeter for him, knowing that if his conscience got the better of him, it would end.

But no decision *is* a decision—a decision to allow circumstances to be in control. Mitch's procrastination allowed fate to make the next move,

which led to a set of events neither of us antici-
pated.

One night when the band was taking a break, I
saw Ace talking to a man near the stage, whispering loud enough for me to hear.

"I thought I told you not to show up here," Ace
hissed. "I could lose my job."

"Until you come up with the money you owe,
I'll show up anywhere I please," the man said. He
looked like a real treble-maker, the classic maf-
fia guy—black clothes and hat, and puffing on a
cigar.

"I told you, Tony. I'll have the money soon."

"You been tellin' me that for two weeks. You
were desperate to pay your gambling debt. I
loaned you the money. It's time to pay up." He
put his cigar in his mouth and spoke through his
teeth. "You promised you'd have it."

"I feel like I made a deal with the devil, dis-
guised as a loan shark. You're fleecing me with
the interest."

Tony raised his voice. "You agreed to it."

I was sitting close enough that Ace could have
reached out and touched me. It was strange, getting this information so easily. I would have made
a perfect stool pigeon if I could talk.

"Shhh! I don't want to discuss it here." Ace's
voice was intense, scared.

"You don't have a choice. It's the only place I
can corner you," Tony said. "Listen, you have the

money for me by Saturday or you gonna disappear and no one'll know where you went."

The muscles in Ace's jaw rolled around as he clenched his teeth. He closed his eyes and took a long breath through his nose. Looking back at Tony, he said, "I need more time. Give me another week."

"I've given you all the time you gonna get. Saturday, you hear? You know where to find me. And by the way, don't think about skipping the country or you'll find yourself floating face-down in the river." Tony scanned the room with an alert focus, then moved through the crowd and out the door.

Neither guessed a guitar could eavesdrop, not that it mattered. I couldn't tell anyone, nor could I help Ace—or so I thought. Right after Tony left, Ace turned and looked at me. I had a gut-string feeling that sent chills up my rosewood back. Instinctively, I became wary, my strings taut. Ace had dollar signs in his eyes! I realized I *could* help him. But who could help me?

After the break, the band members moved back to their instruments. Mitch put a hand up, speaking to the audience. "I'll be just a moment." He turned to Sal. "I need to retune the guitar. For some strange reason, the strings are sounding sharp, almost as if someone tightened them."

If Mitch only knew that I was the culprit. All at once I missed Joe terribly. He was always in tune with me and knew when the tone of my feelings had changed. Noticing, he would ask what was going on, and then intuitively respond. But Mitch wasn't Joe. Mitch was a good guy, but he wasn't Joe.

When we were done for the night, Mitch said, "Ace, I'm going to hang around for a while. Please put my guitar in the car."

I froze, my body becoming so rigid I thought it would crack. Now that I suspected Ace had designs on me, I didn't want him touching me.

"Sure thing, Mitch," Ace said. He sauntered nonchalantly—too nonchalantly, to the stage to take care of his usual break-down, pack-up duties. When finished, he took me off the stand and began putting me in the case. I internally screamed with everything I had: *Mitch, stop him!* Joe would have heard me, but Mitch kept right on talking to his buddies, clueless.

Humming, and acting as if nothing was different from any other night, Ace closed the case, picked it up and walked out the door. He was not humming when he threw me into the backseat of his car, got in, slammed the door and drove away, leaving everything behind—The Blue Heaven Night Club, Mitch, and his job.

We had come to the repeat sign again—guitar-napped yet another time. My spirits struck an all-time low note. Was it karma from a past life? In my spruce youth, or as a mahogany or rosewood tree, had I done some horrible thing and I was now paying? Trees can't really be bad, can they? They move in the wind, drop leaves and dead branches, but they aren't kidnappers. Maybe I fell and killed someone.

What about guitars? They break a string now and then, but they don't steal, lie or cheat. Maybe in a previous life, I hung out with a banjo. Banjos are bad news. That was probably it.

While I puzzled, Ace drove. He stopped once for gas, then pressed on through the night. The tension in my neck and back left me exhausted, and I dozed. When the car slowed and stopped, I awoke. Ace rustled around in the front seat and then all was quiet, except for the sound of tires rolling on pavement, a honking car now and then, and Ace's snoring. I figured we must be parked alongside a road somewhere in a city.

After what seemed like an eternity, Ace made sounds of getting out of the car and opening the back door. He lifted me out, walked a short distance, stopped, and I heard what sounded like a creaky door. He carried me a bit farther and set me down.

"Hello," said a deep male voice. "May I help you?"

"Yes. I have a prized item I want to hock."

Hock? We must be in a pawn shop.

"Let me see what you've got," the man said.

Ace took me out of the case and immediately my body was flooded with a musty smell. Although the room was poorly lit, I could see many items hanging, or sitting on dusty ledges. Jewelry was grouped on a shelf under a glass counter separate from another one holding knives and guns. On the wall behind the counter a sign read, "Jerry's Pawn and Loan." Jerry was a short man with brown curly hair, who looked to be in his mid-thirties.

"This is a guitar, made by the famous Victor Marcini, who has passed away. Since his death the value of his guitars has been steadily rising."

"It's a beauty, alright. Where'd you get it?" asked Jerry.

"It belonged to Maricini's son who sold it to me when he came into hard times. Now I've come into hard times."

A lie! Falsetto information! I was fuming. The number of people claiming to have bought me from Joe were piling up. The truth was that no selling had taken place. And the one who had come into hard times was me.

"I want to hock the guitar just until I've taken care of my cash flow problems. Then I'll be back to get it."

More falsetto information. After he paid Tony, he'd skip the country.

Ace continued. "I know I'm taking my chances here in Nashville. Any musician who sees it is going to want it."

Ahh. So we were in Nashville. I'd heard it was called Music City. I knew names like Chet Atkins, Glen Miller, Hank Williams, and Duke Ellington who had played here. Mitch was a big fan of Duke Ellington. Did Mitch ever travel to Nashville? Would he think to look for me here? I thought the chances were slim. The truth of my fate alarmed me. To release the tension, I popped a string.

"What just happened?" Jerry asked. "One of the strings broke."

"Yeah. A minor problem," said Ace.

"When you've fixed it, we'll talk."

Ace found an extra set of strings in the case, and replaced my broken one.

Then he turned expectantly toward Jerry, who said, "I'll give you one hundred."

"Impossible," squawked Ace. "You can easily sell it for four hundred. Any musician who knows guitars will see the value of this one. Some will recognize it as a Marcini guitar." Ace's body straightened. "I need at least three fifty."

"Three fifty? Impossible. It will never sell for that price. I grant you, it is a beautiful guitar. I'll give you two hundred."

"I can't let it go for that. You need to understand this is a Marcini. A one-of-a-kind Marcini.

The value of your whole shop will go up just by having it displayed here."

Jerry pressed his lips together. He picked me up and ran his fingers up and down my neck, then strummed. His body and face relaxed. It seemed my magic was affecting him.

"Two hundred fifty and that's final," he said. "I've never paid that much for a guitar, so if you're planning on leaving it here, I suggest you accept the offer."

"Way less than what it's worth, but okay." Ace went to the counter and filled out the paperwork. "I'll be back for it."

He became a blur as he took the money and hurried out the door. Just like that, I was relegated to a dark pawn shop dungeon.

Jerry put a three hundred twenty five dollar price tag on me and found a place near the door where I could be seen easily by anyone who came into the shop.

And there I sat. And sat. And sat. And sat. Days went by. Then weeks. People entered and left the shop. Some showed interest, but when they saw the cost, they asked to look at less expensive guitars.

Unlike other guitars in the shop, I needed stimulation. As time crawled, I counted to ten thousand in three different languages, composed sonnets, and imagined the works of some of the great composers.

One day I amused myself by reviewing some of the fairy tales I'd heard Joe's parents read to him as a child. I ran through the stories of *Hansel and Gretel*, *Snow White*, and *Cinderella*. When I came to *Rapunzel,* I envisioned myself being the imprisoned princess, but it was hard. This musty shop was not a castle and even if I had long blond hair, who would rescue me? I moved on to *Sleeping Beauty* and an idea hit me. Could I put myself into a deep sleep? What a relief that would be! I knew sometimes I could take myself away from my misery by meditating. My magic couldn't give me legs to walk out of the shop, but maybe I could get away from the boredom by putting myself to sleep. I saw no prince on the horizon, so what would it matter if I slept for a hundred years?

I decided to try. I imagined it was my sixteenth birthday. I was up in a small room at the top of a castle looking at the old woman with her spinning wheel. The bad fairy carried me over to the spinning wheel where the needle pricked my neck.

𝄞 ♪ Chapter 20

I *didn't know* I had fallen asleep until a man caressed my spruce top and then lifted me from the guitar stand. I was disoriented and couldn't remember where I was. Then I saw the sign—Jerry's Pawn and Loan. Hanging on the wall was a calendar with a blonde woman who had more curves than I did. Under the picture was the name, Marilyn Monroe. The month was June, the year, 1975. What? 1975? I looked at the man standing below the sign. It was Jerry, but he had gray hair! Recognition flooded my memory. Sleeping-Rose Beauty hadn't slept a hundred years, but she had slept twenty-five—long enough for Jerry to become an old man.

"I know this guitar!" the man holding me marveled. "I can't believe it is sitting here in a pawn shop!" Was this stranger my prince, bringing me awake from my deep sleep? Cobwebs were crisscrossed in my hollow body and I had a few in my thoughts, as well. Who was he?

"This beauty was made by Victor Marcini," he said.

"*Yes, yes! That's me,*" I wanted to shout.

A man next to him said, "How do you know, Jake?"

"I visited Marcini's shop years ago. I recognize this particular guitar, not just because of the fine craftsmanship, but because the soundhole is heart-shaped, and black spider webbing runs down the back. Also, for some reason I remember noticing it had five silver screws and one gold one in the pegs."

His companion looked closely at my head. "I'll be darned! You're right!"

"We came here to find you a better guitar, Lester, but it won't be this one," said Jake. "I wasn't in the market for a guitar, but this one is going to be mine. I wanted to buy it when I first saw it, but Mr. Marcini said he made it for his son, so it wasn't for sale."

"It's all yours," said Lester. "I'm going to look around."

My cobweb-impaired memory reached back in time. This guy looked familiar. Who was he? My thoughts stirred around through the fuzz until a light dawned. I had it! Jake DeGarmo, the country-folk singer. I remember his disappointment when he was told I wasn't for sale. He was so much younger then, just a kid. Now his face was weathered and his trimmed beard showed a hint of gray.

Jerry came from behind the counter. "I've had the guitar for a long time. It's a swell piece of work, but the cost has put people off. I originally paid two fifty for it, which in today's prices would be more. For a long time, I was asking three twenty five, and then I lowered it to two seventy five. After a while I gave up thinking I'd ever sell it. Pay me what I paid—two hundred fifty, and it's yours."

Jake didn't bother to counter-offer. "Sold," he said. He dusted my neck and shoulders with his hand. "I don't know that you've ever played it, but this guitar has an amazing sound. Let me purchase a new set of strings to put on, and I'll demonstrate while my buddy looks around."

I was wide awake now. With Jake as my prince, I was once again ready to dazzle the world.

After Jake replaced my strings, he asked Jerry, "How did this guitar come into your hands?"

"A guy came in here saying he had bought it from Marcini's son, who was having money problems. He told me he'd be back for it right away. His life must have gone a different direction. I never saw him again." Jerry gave a short laugh and continued. "The guy asked four hundred. I thought, 'No way!'" He shook his head. "But the $250 I paid was more than I'd ever paid for a guitar up to that time." He lowered his voice. "I didn't expect to feel this way, but when I picked it up and held it, I wanted it for myself. I know it sounds crazy because I don't even play, but it has a warm vibe I can actually feel."

"*Yes*," I wanted to shout. "*It's because I'm alive!*"

The owner continued. "I was sure someone would see its value and buy it."

"I know what you mean," said Jake. "There's a magical quality to it. I came under its spell those many years ago."

I was getting happier by the minute. Jake probably didn't believe in my magic, but he was clearly feeling it.

"Lucky for me, others were put off by the price," Jake said. He settled on a wooden chair in the corner. "I'll play one of my own songs."

"Your own song?" Jerry asked. "Are you a performer?"

Lester turned from where he was looking at guitars. "You haven't heard of him? Jake DeGarmo?"

"Oh, DeGarmo. Yes, I have," said Jerry. "You're Jake DeGarmo?"

"Yeah. I haven't hit the big lights, but I've been around for years, doing my own concerts and opening for big names," said Jake. "We call ourselves The Garma Boys. There are three of us. Ed, who is out in our bus, plays bass."

"I see." Jerry paused. "Garma—from your last name."

"Right," Jake said.

"What kind of a bus?" Jerry asked.

"It's one we fixed up to be our traveling music bus. We live in it from March through October, going from place to place. I spend the winter at my home in Knoxville, writing songs."

Lester interrupted. "Have you heard 'That's the Way It Is on the radio?"

"Yes, it's been on the charts for quite awhile now, sung by James Taylor," said Jerry.

"Well, that is a song Jake wrote," said Lester.

"Impressive," said Jerry.

So Jake was a songwriter and other people sang his songs. Maybe he would write one about me. Certainly a song about me would hit the charts right away.

"So what's it like living on the road?" asked Jerry.

I was wondering the same thing. My future life was being discussed here.

"It can be a little grueling at times. But all in all, it's a life many musicians only dream of."

"Where are you playing next? Maybe I can come see you."

"It will be right here in Nashville. Ed does our scheduling. He will be putting up some flyers around the city, but also, our gigs will be announced on the radio."

He looked down at me, smiled, and slid his hand up my neck.

"I'll be playing this guitar at our next show." He pointed at his friend. "Lester plays backup guitar. We've been together a long time. We make a good team."

He began to sing and play his song, "Life in the Slow Lane." I was enthralled with how quickly I responded to his nimble fingers. Asleep so long, I almost forgot who I was. Jake coaxed me into my full glorious resonance. I put forth every bit of charm I could, showing him he was making a good decision.

Feeling the wonderful vibes in my body once again made me think of Joe. Like Jerry, Joe must be an older man now. Did he think of me? Would I ever see him again, or would my memory of him continue to fade into the foggy past? I felt a twinge of sadness, but then I came back to the clarity of the present moment.

Fully awake and feeling frisky after my years of impoundment, I couldn't wait to get out of the pawn shop. The beginning of the third movement of the symphony of my life began coursing through my body. I was ready to swing into a light-hearted scherzo.

Before we left, Lester found the guitar he wanted and paid for it. Jake stuffed me inside a musty case, and we were on our way.

Outside, Jake said, "I forgot where the Ritz is parked."

I was puzzled. The Ritz? What did he mean?

"Around the corner," said Lester.

A few steps later, a door opened. Jake slid me in and the door closed. Aha! This was The Ritz. I was Rose, the guitar. This was Ritz, the bus.

"Hi Ed. Hope you're not tired of waiting. We hit a gold mine in there. It took awhile."

"It's okay," said Ed. "I took a nap."

"Let's head back to the park and spend some time jamming," said Jake. "We'll need to make a song list and work on that one song we're having trouble with."

Yikes! We were going to a park? As bad memories rushed in, my heart began beating in cut time. *Chill, Rose, chill.* I wasn't with Roy and Barney. I mustn't superimpose the past over the present. That was then. This was now.

"Yeah, and I'm excited to try out my new guitar," said Lester.

As the bus slowly picked up speed, Jake said, "Lester, can you get my purchase out of its case and hand it to me?"

Yay! I was getting out. My curiosity had been eating away at me.

Jake took me from Lester and said, "Look at this guitar, Ed! I can't believe it's mine!"

Ed glanced my way. "Well, I'm driving right now, but I can see it is made from beautiful wood."

I checked out my surroundings. A closer look revealed that the bus had a cooking/sitting area, and three beds. Tight quarters, but a home on wheels.

Ed spoke. "We'll be in Nashville for at least a couple of weeks. I've lined up some places for us to play—a couple of restaurant-bars and we lucked out by getting into the National Music Festival at Fitzgerald Park next Saturday. It has been advertised for weeks. One of the bands backed out. I talked to the organizer and he put us in.

"Cool, Ed. It's what we pay you the big bucks for, you know. You have connections."

"Ha! Why haven't I seen any of these big bucks?"

Jake began strumming me, playing various runs and chord progressions.

"A gold mine is right," said Ed. "That guitar has an unusually sweet, mellow tone. You lucked out."

"You don't know the whole story," said Jake. "When I was in my twenties just getting started in music, I saw this very guitar in Marcini's workshop. Victor Marcini was a well-known luthier at the time."

"I can't believe you would have remembered that particular guitar after all this time," said Ed.

"I know. I'm surprised, too. I don't understand it, but I was drawn to it the first time I saw it, and the minute I laid my eyes on it in the pawn shop, I recognized it."

I listened, fascinated. By this time in my life, I had come to realize that beyond my beautiful body and sounds, I had a charisma that attracted people to me—part of the magic that came through Victor's hands when he first brought me into this world. But at first, I didn't know what charisma was. It didn't have a sound or a look. I discovered it through the mirror of others. I was comforted, knowing that because people were drawn to me, I would always be loved no matter where I was. I hoped Heaven was a real place, and that someday, I could find Victor there and thank him for the gifts he had given me.

"How do you like the guitar you bought, Lester?" asked Ed.

"It's nothing like the one Jake got, but it will be perfect for our shows. I think I can get a deeper resonance from it than my other one."

"I'd call it a successful venture into the city then," said Ed.

Buildings and cars thinned as we moved into the outskirts of Nashville. Eventually, we came to the park Ed had spoken of. He was able to put us on the grass in a beautiful spot facing a small pond. In minutes, an awning was erected on the side of the bus. Chairs were put out and as we sat in the afternoon quiet, with Jake still plucking my strings, I got a good look at the outside of the bus. Its background color was a light blue. An oversized guitar was painted on the side, and above it was the name of the band, written in large letters: The Garma Boys.

As Jake played with my strings, the other two engaged in conversation.

"So tell us about our first gig, Ed," said Lester.

"We'll be at the Captain's Bar on First Avenue tomorrow night."

"We need to get some new songs going—add some variety," said Lester.

"Yeah, the audience likes variety," said Ed. "That's why you guys are such a hit." He smirked.

"Your looks provide plenty of variety. Lester, you're as ugly as a toad and Jake is an All-American male beauty."

Lester laughed.

"What about you, Ed?" said Jake. "You are a squatty seed pod with a head on top and feet at the bottom." They couldn't stop laughing. Nor could I. My body was shaking and my sides were about to split. Jake was too involved in his own laughing to notice. This kind of humor was new to my experience. The dynamics with these three musicians was light, upbeat, friendly. Until now, I hadn't realized I had a funny bone, but evidently, I did. Their exaggerations, laced with an edge of truth, were cracking me up.

I looked at Lester with amused affection. His nose was too big for his face, his chin too small, and his curly reddish hair way out of control. But he didn't seem to care. Maybe after looking in the mirror a few times, he said, "There's nothing I can do here. I'll move on to something else." I didn't know him well, but it seemed with his easy smile and the way he draped his body on the chair, he was comfortable inside his own body, completely at home with himself. I found this to be quite attractive.

Jake probably took his turn and Lester's in front of the mirror. I would have if I were him. Even considering his age, Jake had a youthful boyish look to him. His clean, graying hair hung straight to his shoulders and blended well with his trimmed beard. His sculpted nose was in proportion with his face, and blue eyes sparkled under crescent-shaped eyebrows. He probably sent the decibels of women's heartbeats off the chart each time he performed. I wondered if he'd ever been married.

"Let's go through our songs for tomorrow night," said Jake. "And Lester, you can try out the guitar you bought."

The first song was "Peaceful, Easy Feeling," by the Eagles. Because I'd slept through the sixties, I'd never heard it. But no matter. Unlike Jake, I was not required to memorize words, learn chords, or practice. I could sit and look pretty, with not a care in the world, while Jake focused on perfecting his musicianship. All I had to do was supply the tones he needed to make him sound good. He did the work while I played.

On the chorus, Ed, Lester, and Jake sang in harmony, with a tight blending that sent me to the moon. It was the first time I'd participated in these kinds of vocal vibrations.

When the song ended, Ed said, "Wow! I love the way we did that song."

"Well, I love this guitar," said Jake. "Funny thing. It seems like it is responding to me. I know that sounds crazy, but it feels like we are partners in creating the sounds."

"Whatever the two of you are doing, it sounds awesome," said Ed. "Is it my imagination or did that song sound better than it ever has?'

"I'm sure of it," said Lester. "I wonder why?"

"It's the guitar, Lester," said Jake.

"We'll see," said Ed. "As we go through the rest of our songs, if they all sound better, we'll know it's your guitar, Jake."

I wanted to say, "You've hit the peg on the head. I'm the queen-pin here."

Jake looked at Lester. "How was your guitar? Is it working for you?"

"It's not responding to me, Jake. Maybe I should take it back. I'm not feeling the magic. It's just lying here in my arms, sounding like a normal guitar." Ed and Jake laughed.

"But yeah, I like it."

"Let's run through 'The House of New Orleans,'" said Jake. "I'm going to get out my pick."

Not long after we began, Jake's pick flipped from between his finger and thumb and flew through my soundhole.

"Dang! My pick just went inside the guitar."

"Well, shake it out," said Lester.

Jake turned me upside down and began shaking. The pick was popping around like a pinball.

"*Stop! Stop!*" I wanted to yell. "*You are messing up my harmonics.*"

Jake kept shaking. "I can't get it to come out."

167

"Here. Let me try," said Lester.

Lester shook me even harder than Jake. What an idiot! Harder wasn't what was needed. It was a matter of aligning the pick with the hole. I felt like I'd just swallowed a woodpecker that was joyfully pounding holes in my sides.

"Okay, let me try again," said Jake. After more wild shaking, I'd had enough. I focused my energy and spit the offending piece of plastic out the opening. It smacked Jake on the forehead.

"Did you see that?" exclaimed Jake.

"What?" said Lester. "You got the pick out, I see."

"No. It came shooting out of the hole on its own, and hit me in the head."

"Yeah, and while that was going on, my guitar was flying around."

"That's fine. Don't believe me, but that's what happened."

"Don't get bent out of shape, Jake," said Ed. "Let's get going on the song."

And just like that, my pick-spitting act was forgotten. Jake did what most humans do when faced with an unexplainable situation. He blotted it out and got back to the comfort of his own beliefs. As long as I no longer had a pick in my belly, I didn't care what Jake believed.

I was in love with the sharp clear sounds that came from my strings as Jake skillfully picked the background arpeggios of "The House of New Orleans."After a few more songs, the three stopped for a short dinner. With energy high, we continued on into the night.

Yes, we sounded great. They all agreed that I must be the reason. People were going to love us. I was jazzed.

🎼 Chapter 21

We arrived at the Captain's Bar the next night with my curiosity making it hard for me to lie still in the case. My fidgety body was relieved when Jake finally took me out and put me on a stand.

The placement of the stage at the Captain's Bar was something I had never seen. It was flush with the bottom of a big front window, three feet off the floor. To my surprise, the window was wide open, which meant people walking by on the sidewalk would hear us.

With backs to the window, facing the people seated at the bar and tables, Jake was standing, while Lester and Ed sat on either side of him. Each had a microphone. A tall man came up to the stage. "Welcome. We're glad you're here."

"I'm Jake, and you must be Al." said Jake.

"Yes. Do you need anything?"

No," Jake replied. "I think we're ready to roll."

Yes, I was ready to roll. It had been a long time since I'd been in front of an audience. I wanted people to see me, hear me, love me.

We used the set list we'd gone through the night before, beginning with a Bob Dylan song, moving on to The Who, Elvis Presley, and Credence Clearwater. Jake also sang a couple of his own songs. Some of the songs he sang alone, but when the three sang together, I got chills up my back. This was a different kind of harmony than I'd heard in the past, where various instruments played together, or even where the sound of my own strings were in a delightful relationship with one another. Here we were with instruments and voices all blending on the same euphoric wave length.

Partway through the evening, I heard someone on the sidewalk say, "These guys are great! Let's go in and listen."

Two men entered and sat at the bar.

Not long after that, I heard a woman outside the window say, "What band is this? I haven't heard them. Let's have dinner here." A man and woman entered and stood at the door waiting to be seated.

A short while later, a deep voice from behind us said, "My feet are refusing to take me on down the sidewalk. This music is unbelievable. Do you mind if we stop?"

Another male voice said, "No, no. This is fine. We wanted to find some good music tonight. Here it is."

Throughout the evening more and more people entered the restaurant until no more seating was available. When we took a ten minute break, Al walked over to the stage and said, "What kind of magic is going on? You've filled the place. Your harmonies are great, and I can't get enough of that guitar, Jake."

There was that word again: Magic. More people had come under my spell. My heart felt like it was doing cartwheels. The only time I'd been happier was when I was with Joe. *Joe, Joe, Joe. Where are you?*

I yanked myself back. Thinking about Joe was causing a rain on my parade, and the parade of people coming into the restaurant was something to be celebrated. I was the queen of this parade.

We started our next set, and not once did I see anyone leave. After the last song, everyone clapped and cheered and yelled, "More, more!" We played an encore and then Jake said to everyone, "Thank you for your wonderful response. You have been a great audience."

Al stepped forward. "You are welcome here any time. I'd love to book another gig."

Ed spoke. "Thanks. We'd like that. I'll get back to you."

On our way out, I heard a woman's voice. "I could listen to your guitar all day. I can't say exactly why I like it so much, but I was mesmerized the whole evening. I hope you will come back." She laughed. "And bring the guitar, please."

Headed back to the park, it sounded like a crowd of people were inside the Ritz. Ed, Jake, and Lester, with elevated voices, were all talking at the same time. I was being given most of the credit for the success of the evening. Elevated by their excitement, I let their words flow in and around me like bubbling champagne.

The following Friday night, we entered Horseshoe Haven, the next place Ed had set up for us. As we passed through a sea of talking and laughing, I was so excited I began to jiggle around.

Jake said, "That's funny. It feels like people are bumping the case, but no one is near us."

"Maybe instead of a guitar, you have a wild cat in there." Lester laughed.

I toned down. Any concerns Jake might have about me always evaporated as soon as I went back to acting like a normal guitar.

He walked a ways farther, took me out and placed me on a stand. Free again! We were on a good-sized stage at the end of a long room. A large dance floor separated us from the dinner tables. The bar was beyond the tables, near the entrance. I was sitting on the edge of my stand with excitement.

This was a music-loving city, and word of mouth was a wonderful thing. All those voices I heard came from a packed house, and naturally, it was because of me. We were advertised on the radio and Ed put up posters around the city, which allowed my new fan club to invite friends and find their way to the next place where they could hear the magic guitar. I knew I was pretty full of myself, but who could argue with the evidence? Look at the crowd that had gathered. I had no trouble accepting with grace-notes that which could not be denied: I was a phenomenon.

We repeated many of the same numbers we'd done at the Captain's Bar, but also added new ones. Again, Jake sang some of his own. Clapping and whistling followed each number. On the songs in which the rhythm invited dancing, people crowded the floor. I was in my element.

When it was time to leave, a big man came to the stage. He shook Ed's hand. "They call me Tennessee Ted, or just Ted. I'm the owner here. Your performance was absolutely phenomenal. We hope you will book with us again."

"Thanks, Ted. We'll be in touch."

Going back to the park, the Ritz once again was filled with excited chatter. I wanted to join in, but not able to do that, my elation built until one of my strings popped.

Jake said, "What was that?"

"I think one of the strings on your guitar broke," said Lester.

"Weird. I put on new strings at the pawn shop—my last package." He paused. "It's okay. Let's find a music store tomorrow and I'll replace it and buy another backup set."

As high as Jake was, it was clear a broken string couldn't dampen his spirits.

The following afternoon, as we headed for the city, Ed said, "After we find a music store, let's check out the stage where the music festival is being held next Saturday."

"Good plan," Lester said. "How many bands are playing?"

"Not sure," said Ed. "Maybe six or seven. It should be a full day of great music. I want to hear some of the other groups they have lined up."

We began stopping at traffic lights, so I knew we were back in the city.

"Slow down," Lester said. "I see a music store ahead. On the right, Ed. See it? It's called Guitars and More."

"Yeah. And we can park right in front," said Ed.

After we entered the music store, Jake set down the case I was in and said, "Hi. We're just in for a guitar string. Maybe you could put it on for us."

"Hello. I'm Bart. Which string do you need replaced?"

"The D," said Jake.

He opened the case, pulled me out and what I saw shocked me so much I immediately popped two more strings. The boy working in the shop was a dead ringer for Joe when I last saw him. I knew I must be hallucinating, so I took another look, and then in astonishment I popped all the rest of my strings. What was going on? It wasn't Joe. Of course it wasn't Joe. He would have aged by now. Who was this look-alike? My pulse was moving in double time.

"Good grief! This is the strangest thing I've ever seen," said Jake. "This guitar seems to have a mind of its own and has decided to get all of its strings replaced."

Bart laughed. "You're right. Pretty crazy. Bring her to me and we will do as she wishes."

Bart was talking like I was an entity, not an "it." He picked me up and looked closely. After rubbing his hand over my back and sides he said with wonderment, "Where did you get this guitar? I have one that looks almost exactly like it."

"I bought it in a pawn shop, but it once belonged to Joe Marcini."

"What?" said Bart. "That's my father! Are you telling me this is the guitar that my grandpa made for my dad—the guitar that was stolen?"

I needed to tone down. I was getting so excited I was about to explode into splinters. Joe had a son?

"I didn't know it was stolen," said Jake. "Like I said, I found it in a pawn shop here in Nashville. I remembered it from when I visited Victor's shop many years ago."

"I'm blown away. What are the chances you would end up here with my dad's guitar?"

"You mean what used to be your dad's guitar," Jake said defensively. "It's mine now."

"I hear what you're saying," said Bart, "but really, she is still my dad's guitar.

Jake took a deep breath. "No, actually, I don't think so."

At a standstill, I wanted to cast the deciding vote.

But Jake's voice eased—probably because he knew his advantage: As things stood, I was his. "Tell me how the guitar was stolen."

"In New Orleans, there was a guy that hated my dad. He quit the band at Mayfield's Jazz Bar after my dad joined it, and then came back a few days later and stole the guitar." Bart threw one hand up in the air. "My dad was devastated."

"That's understandable. I didn't know about that part of the guitar's history."

"Anyway, my grandpa made the guitar especially for my dad, and they both felt it had a magic to it."

Jake smiled. "Yeah. I can see how they would think that. It's a pretty special guitar."

"When the guitar was stolen, Dad told me he felt like his heart had been torn out."

Me too, me too! I wanted to yell.

Bart looked back at a case behind him. "My dad made me a guitar just like this one. The only thing my guitar doesn't have is a gold screw. I'm not sure what the story is on that. I'll have to ask."

I know the story. I can tell you, I wanted to say.

He pulled the case up onto the counter. "I take my guitar with me everywhere I go. Want to see it?"

"Yes," said Jake. "This whole story is unbelievable."

True. Unbelievable in many ways. I could see my life circling around, bringing me back to where I began.

Bart opened the case and pulled out a guitar that was my twin—the only difference being that one gold screw I still had in the peg in my head. I could only stare. Immediately I began to feel uncomfortable, like an only child that has had all the attention, but now must share it. Bart began strumming. I didn't want to admit it, but the guitar sounded pretty good.

Just like Victor, Joe had made a guitar for his son. Surely, he put all the love he felt for his son, but also for me, into the guitar as he made it. And now here it was and it looked just like me. I suppose I should have been touched with the beautiful sentiment of it all, but I was filled with an ugly jealousy—a tense unfamiliar feeling. I was always the favored one, standing out from all other guitars—the queen of guitars. And now here was this imposter, looking and sounding as good as me. I was so keyed up I wanted to pop more strings, but I'd used them all up.

"Beautiful!" said Jake. "And you play well. Was your dad the teacher?"

"Yes. We play together all the time now."

Not fair, not fair, I wanted to scream. I hated this guitar. She got to be near Joe all these years while I was moving around the South from one owner to the next. Not fair, not fair.

"How have you come to be at this music store?" asked Jake.

"My girlfriend lives in Nashville. I'm here for the summer so I can spend more time with her."

Another customer stepped through the door.

"Go ahead and help him. We can wait," said Jake.

When the customer left, Bart asked, "What are your names?"

"I'm Jake, this is Ed and Lester."

"I'm confused about my feelings," said Bart. "I'm glad to know that my dad's guitar ended up with some good guys, but I wish it could be back in his hands."

Exactly! I was not at all confused. I belonged with Joe. Period.

"I can't blame you," said Jake.

"I wonder if I can talk you into selling it back to him," Bart said.

Jake didn't miss a beat. "Not a chance," he said. "I'm really sorry it was stolen from your dad, but that was many years ago. We are feeling the magic of the guitar in our performances. The response has been amazing. I have absolutely no interest in selling it."

Each word Jake spoke sent a spike of pain through my heart.

"I'm sorry to hear that," said Bart. "What a shame to actually find the guitar my dad loved so much, but not be able to reunite him with it. At least give it some thought. We could work out a deal where you could have one of my dad's other very fine, well-made guitars."

"I can't imagine wanting any other guitar than this one," said Jake.

Being loved by Jake and his friends had given me a feeling of peace and security, but now that security felt like tethers on my soul.

"Change of subject here. If you're free next Saturday, we will be playing at the Nashville Music Festival," said Ed. "We are called the Garma Boys. You should come by."

"I was planning on going to the festival. I've already asked for the day off," said Bart.

"Great. We hope to see you there," said Ed.

Bart picked me up. Heartbreak was in his voice as he said, "One more time, I'm appealing to your altruistic side. Please give some thought to our discussion. By choosing one of Joe's other guitars, one just as good as this one, everyone benefits."

"Sorry," Jake said. "I'm set with this one."

Bart restrung me, Jake bought a set of backup strings, and we left.

Not only was I still filled with jealousy, I was bereft. We were losing touch with the only possible contact I had that would take me back to Joe. I thought things were going in that direction, and then Jake refused to budge. "No," he said. "Absolutely not," he said. I wanted to pitch a fit—bang my body on a floor somewhere and scream, but instead I laid in the dark case, aching like I did when I was first stolen, and feeling like I was once again being kidnapped.

Chapter 22

The following Saturday, we were not scheduled to play until two, but we showed up at ten because Jake, Ed, and Lester wanted to listen to the other bands. I was in the case, so I could hear, but not see. The three began talking about the first band on stage.

"This group reminds me of some of the ones I heard down in New Orleans," said Jake. "Great sax player."

"I don't think the guitar player is as good as you are, Jake," said Lester. "But then he doesn't have the guitar you have."

"Oh? You think this guitar plays itself?"

Lester laughed. "Yeah. I think it does. I think you're just faking your finger moves."

"Ha!" said Jake. "Just pay attention to your own fingers, Les, because they're going to have a hard time keeping up. This guitar and I are going to tear up this place today."

It was true. We would. I was sure of it. Jake's expertise was the doorway I needed to create my enchanting music, and my magic was the doorway Jake needed to "tear up the place." Together we would charm the crowd. I knew Joe's son would be there, but I didn't want to think about that. Too painful.

Throughout the morning, Jake, Lester and Ed sometimes wandered around and sometimes rested, as they listened to the different bands. I could hear people's chatter and children's laughter. Time passed. I got restless.

Finally, Ed said, "We go on in a half hour. Let's tune up."

I was relieved. The waiting was over. When we were nearer to the music, Jake pulled me out of the case. I tried not to sigh my relief too loud. No need to get everyone wondering.

Many people were sitting on blankets in a large grassy area. Around the edges were food booths. Parents sat in chairs under the trees watching their children do somersaults .

A man came up to the side of the stage where we were waiting. "You must be the Garma Boys," he said.

"Yes, that's us," said Jake.

Do you need anything?"

"No, I think we're set."

The people on stage played their last number, the crowd applauded, and as they left the stage, we entered. I was jittery-bug excited.

When we were set and ready to go, Jake looked out at the audience and said, "We are the Garma Boys. I'm Jake. Lester, on my right, is backup guitar and this is Ed, our bass player. We're glad to be here. Let's get started."

We began with Jimmy Buffet's "Margaritaville," and followed with "Proud Mary." A rowdy chorus of voices filled the air as people sang along. This was my first music festival. I could see why people gathered at such events. Music is a language of communion, a language of the heart. I saw that its positive effect increased when experienced in this large group of music lovers. In their regular lives, many of these people would probably not associate with one another, but here in the park, they were brothers and sisters, bonded by this common experience of joy. As we began the last verse, I saw warmth, and yes, love, radiating from everyone—a crowd of people all wearing *rose* colored glasses, our magical music spreading over them like a summer rain.

We continued with "Light My Fire" by the Doors. The people responded with enthusiasm.

Then I saw Joe.

My world stopped. If I'd had a mouth, it would have been hanging wide open. I could feel Jake's frustration as my strings loosened and the volume muted. When the song ended, he said to our listeners, "Excuse us a minute. We need to make a few minor adjustments."

"What's going on, Jake?" asked Ed. "Something must have happened to your microphone."

A stage hand tapped it. "Nope. Nothing wrong here," he said.

"I don't know what's going on," said Jake. "I couldn't believe how good we sounded, and then all at once the guitar went mute."

"Quite puzzling," said Ed. "A guitar doesn't just go mute."

Ed and Jake continued to discuss my poor performance, but I didn't hear them. I was reveling on that beautiful face—a face now covered with a beard; an older face, but still the most beautiful face I had ever seen. I could feel that familiar magnetism that existed between us. I wanted Joe to touch me, hold me.

"We have to keep going," said Lester. "Let's continue and see what happens." I decided to give the best performance of my life—for Joe. Jake strummed the first chord of "I'm a Believer," saw that somehow the problem was resolved, gave Ed a nod, and we launched into the song. The crowd went wild, jumping up and down, singing, dancing, laughing. The whole time that I was giving the best performance of my life, I was watching Joe. His eyes were focused on me, and even from a distance, I could see they were twinkling.

When our time on stage was up, and we'd played our last song, the crowd chanted and applauded, begging for one more. We gave them "Me and Bobby McGee." Arms laid on one another's shoulders while the crowd swayed and sang. I'd never experienced group emotion like this. We were the catalysts for a special happening in this park today.

As we exited, I looked out and saw Joe. He was smiling and walking with Bart toward the stage.

"Hi Jake," said Bart. "Meet my dad, Joe. I invited him up for the concert today."

"Glad to meet you, Joe," said Jake. "... for the second time. I first saw you in your father's workshop, and we were both much younger." He turned and with an open hand indicated his friends. "This is Lester and Ed."

"Nice to meet you," said Joe. "That was a primo performance. Everyone was swept up in the beauty and energy of the music."

His voice! His wonderful deep voice. I could listen to it for hours.

"Thanks," said Jake. "We had a good time."

"It's been so long since I've held that guitar, I wonder if I could just strum a few chords on it."

I was overcome with raw desire. Could Joe see it? I thought so.

"You are welcome to do that." He paused. "Just don't get too attached."

"Hey, Dad. Let's move to the edge of the park where we won't disturb the next band," said Bart.

"Good idea," said Joe.

We stopped under a tree at the outskirts of the park. When Jake handed me over to Joe, I felt a peace I hadn't known since the night I was stolen from Mayfield's Jazz Bar. Joy flooded my body. Joe's hands held me with a love and respect that I had longed for these many years. He began to strum, moving his long, talented fingers across my strings. My body, my heart, my head, my back, my sides, my strings, all responded with an outpouring of love that created the most angelic sound I'd ever made, and our hearts once again became one.

The outside world went away. Then Jake's voice broke in. "Sounds good. You play well."

Jake put out his hands, reaching for me, indicating that our time was up. The spell was broken. With his mouth set in a tight straight line, as if holding back tears, Joe slowly lifted my sad body and placed it back in Jake's arms. I had always pictured reuniting with Joe, but never under these poignant circumstances.

Joe cleared his throat. "This guitar has sentimental value. My father made it for me. I can make you one exactly like it."

"I suppose you can, but I have this one," said Jake.

He was being maddeningly unreasonable! I had thought Jake was an okay person, but right now I saw him as a stubborn jerk. I felt like I was in an arranged marriage with the wrong guy.

"In essence, this guitar still belongs to me," said Joe. "It was stolen, so all those who have possessed it since then have held stolen property."

"I understand your reasoning," said Jake. "I feel bad your guitar was stolen, but a lot of time has passed. I found it and bought it, unaware it had been stolen. I have assumed ownership and I intend to keep it."

"Please, Jake. I'm begging you." Joe sounded defeated. His voice had no life in it. "Give serious thought to choosing one of my very fine guitars, or I can even make you one just like this one."

I knew Joe could not make a guitar exactly like me, and I was afraid Jake knew it, too.

"Hm-m. Well, I'll think about it." I could tell Jake was placating Joe so he could end the conversation. And in so doing, end my hopes ... end my joy ... end my dreams ... end my everything.

♪ Chapter 23

Joe and Bart went their way and we went ours. As we headed toward the stage area where the cases were, Ed asked, "Shall we pack up and head back to the Ritz?"

"Yeah. This was a lot of fun, but I'm ready to go," said Lester.

Who cares what we do? I thought. *My life is over.* In my dismal downward glissando, I wished I could throw myself off a bridge. Helpless to actually end my life, I laid in the case, rewinding the part of the afternoon where Joe was holding me. Painful as it was, I couldn't stop thinking about it.

When I'd seen him, I was so surprised, my world stopped. I felt sparks in the air, the familiar magnetism. The rest of the world went away and all I could see was Joe. A few short moments in his arms and it was over. As he gave me up, I felt his pain. It was palpable. This was the end. Good bye. My pain crashed into his pain, causing the air to turn a dark angry red—the color of angst, the color of fear. It seemed invisible to others, but it consumed me.

In all the time I'd spent longing for Joe, I felt hope. Maybe, just maybe, we would be reunited some day. Now my dreams were shattered. I had no reason to carry on. Without Joe, I was an empty shell. I'd thought that my beauty and magic were important to my joy, but no. Without the completion of the circle of love between us, it hit me that these qualities meant nothing. If it were required of me to give them up in order to be with Joe, I would do it in a heartbeat.

What? Really? This amazing insight tumbled through my consciousness, causing things I thought were me to rearrange themselves. In this moment, I realized my beauty and magic were not the real source of my joy. By themselves, they brought me no happiness.

I didn't know it was possible to love Joe more than I already did, but by releasing the energy I expended on my own wonderful qualities, there was more room for loving him. But what was I to do with all this emotion? Joe was not here to receive it. With nowhere to put it, I thought I might burst. I loved Joe terribly. He loved me terribly. I felt we were acting out our own *Romeo and Juliet* tragedy.

The next morning, Ed announced, "I've set up repeat performances at both the Captain's

Bar and Horse Haven. People know us now. We should draw some good crowds."

I didn't care.

Mid-week, Lester, Ed, and Jake set up outside the Ritz for a practice. I didn't care. They worked up a set list and began with Bob Dylan's "Don't Think Twice." This time when Jake picked me up, his fingers felt intrusive. I no longer wanted him touching me.

About halfway through the song, Jake stopped to retune my strings. Again, a short way into the song, Jake tuned me again. The third time he stopped, Ed said, "Can't you get that guitar in tune, Jake? What's the matter?"

"I have no idea," said Jake. "I just get it tuned and then it goes out again."

"Do you need to tighten the tuning pegs?" asked Lester.

"Maybe so," said Jake.

He got out a screw driver and tightened the screws. The group began again. This time when Jake stopped, Ed was irritated.

"Criminy! What's going on?."

"I'm sorry, guys, but I feel like this is not the same guitar. Something is seriously wrong. The sound is dull and flat. I can't get a good tone out of any of the strings."

"Let me see," said Lester. He picked me up and began playing a familiar chord progression.

"Yup!" he said. "Jake is right. This guitar sounds terrible."

Ed nodded in agreement. I didn't care.

"For now, grab your other guitar, Jake. I want to run through these songs."

Thankfully, Jake put me back in my case. Claustrophobia was no longer an issue. The case was my coffin, exactly where I wanted to be. *Bury me, please. Just put me in a hole in the ground. Eventually, my mahogany, spruce, and rosewood will rot and go back into the Earth. Please! I don't want to be here anymore.*

On the night we were scheduled to play at Captain's Bar, Jake said, "I'm taking both guitars. If the Marcini guitar doesn't come through, I'll have a backup."

"I don't know what to think about that guitar," said Lester. "How could it change so much? Did it sit in the sun? Maybe there's moisture in the case."

"No," said Jake. "It hasn't been in the sun, and I checked. The case is dry."

"The audiences have fallen in love with your guitar, Jake," said Ed. "I hope they don't pay too much attention if you change it out."

I didn't care.

We arrived to a full house. "Here they are," I heard someone say. "Wait until you hear them."

Ed, Lester, and Jake took their places on stage, near the window, as before. Jake had me on a strap over his shoulder.

He greeted the crowd. "We're glad to see so many people here tonight. We are the Garma Boys. Let's get started."

They decided to change the beginning song from "Don't Think Twice," to Elvis Presley's "Heartbreak Hotel." Elvis' song was singing to me of my own heartbreak. I could see Jake struggling, trying his best to make me sound good, but with little success. He sang a little louder and touched my strings lightly, letting Lester carry the song. The crowd gave a lukewarm response. I didn't care.

Three songs later, while Jake was switching guitars, I heard someone say, "I thought you said that was supposed to be some kind of a wonderful guitar." Another voice answered. "I don't get it. The other night it was the brightest, most beautiful guitar I'd ever heard."

Jake, Lester, and Ed played and sang throughout the rest of the evening. People responded with polite applause, but as the evening wound down, I heard Jake say, "Half the people are gone. Without the Marcini guitar, we're not what we were the other night."

Needless to say, the evening ended on a sour note. On the way back to the park, the three men talked, their voices full of concern.

"With this guitar, I thought I had a peach, but it has turned out to be a lemon," said Jake.

He thought I was a lemon? I didn't care.

"It's quite puzzling," said Ed. "I'm not quite sure what to think of it."

They talked on about me, but I didn't care. I laid in my case, wishing for oblivion.

The following morning, the talking continued and then it took a turn. Ed's next words brought me wide awake.

"Jake, maybe you should reconsider Joe's offer. He said he could make you a guitar just like this one."

"I've been thinking about that, too," said Jake. "But what if that one turns out to be a dud, too?"

Lester spoke. "I don't think the guitar Joe makes for you will be a dud. For some reason or other, this guitar works for Joe and not for us. It has not sounded good since he played it, and for no apparent reason that I can see, but certainly it's a fluke that won't happen again."

"Yes, I suppose you're right. Since this guitar is no longer of any use to me, what do I have to lose?"

I cared.

"How about we cancel the Horse Haven gig and head to New Orleans?" said Ed.

"I agree," said Jake. "Maybe you can line up a show for us where we're not expected to perform with a magic guitar."

Was I dreaming? I pinched my strings togeth-er to see if I was awake. In this small turn of the conversation, I cared—more than I'd cared about anything, ever.

When I was taken from Joe, I gave up. By sur-rendering to my fate, I had inadvertently opened a door—opened up my life again. And there was no mistake about it. I was feeling alive. Good thing I hadn't thrown myself off the bridge.

"How are we going to find Joe?" asked Lester.

"Bart said his dad was able to buy the house that he grew up in. He is using the same work-shop his dad used," said Jake. "It's been a long time, but I've been there and I'm sure I can find it."

All night long I tossed and turned in the case. In the morning, I could hear the overhanging tarp being rolled up and the banging of chairs as they were folded and put into the Ritz.

"I think we have everything," said Ed. "Let's boogie out of here."

I thought we would never get to New Orle-ans. I couldn't tell night from day. We stopped three times to sleep. I could hear Jake and Lester jamming while Ed drove. These happy travelers were in no hurry. I was impatient, but it was an impatience filled with anticipation and excite-ment. Jake, Ed, and Lester were taking me to the home key—the common beginning place where Joe and I were born. I could see the big fireplace with small logs burning; Victor's beautiful guitars hanging on the walls; the radio playing a local station; Victor sawing and sanding; and me, sitting on a stand, waiting for Joe to come home from school.

I remembered being thrilled when Victor finally gave Joe his first lesson, both of them sitting in front of the fireplace. Was I ever surprised at how awful I sounded under Joe's awkward fingers. We finally came through that misery with Joe getting over the initial hump, and improving rapidly. As he practiced, I began to sound better. As our two wills began to merge, we started reading each other's moods. The best thing of all was that the better Joe got, the more he loved me.

Before his guitar lessons began, I liked being around Joe, but we were like two kids enjoying our time together. It took Joe's learning the craft of playing me that created the bond, which grew stronger throughout the rest of the time we were together.

Since then I'd had a crazy life, lonely and miserable, separated from Joe. But now I was going home. I imagined I could hear the expansive, crashing sounds of the grand finale of the symphony of my life—violins, flutes, saxophones, clarinets, French horns, tubas, and timpani drums—*The Song of Rose,* ending in a grandiose magnificent coda. The symphony began when I was separated from Joe, and now was ending as I returned to him.

The first movement, allegro, wild and lively, began when I was whisked away. The music mirrored my confusion and angst, the flutes performing notes in a jumpy, rapid succession, revealing my unsettled emotions. The second movement, andante, expressed loneliness, sorrow and longing. My melancholy brought on full, heavy chords, the cellos providing sad melody lines that wove slowly through the harmony of the other instruments. It seemed the third movement, scherzo, began when I awakened from my long sleep, excited to be on stage again, with a musician who got the people up and dancing. And now, the finale! The orchestra, full and expansive, trumpets blaring, timpani drums crashing, cymbals clanging, was bringing this adventure to an end. I could hear parts of the first three movements being cleverly worked in, making the finale a kind of summary of my perilous journey. I gave a glorious sigh as the coda tied up all the loose ends. I was coming home!

I remembered worrying that Joe and I wouldn't always be together because he would age faster than me. Who would have guessed that we'd be separated when we were both still alive? The time we had spent apart brought into focus what really mattered. Worrying about the future was a painful waste of energy. Now that Joe and I were reuniting, I wasn't going to torment myself with what might be.

I thought about all the living things on Earth. The trees I came from began as sprouts. Joe began as a baby. Sprouts and babies, maturing, growing old, passing on, to be replaced by more sprouts and babies. It was nature's way. Opposing this cycle was pointless. There was nothing that could be done to change it. I could either resist it and suffer, or accept it and be happy. I intended to be happy—to enjoy each precious moment with Joe, made sweeter by the uncertainty of what laid ahead.

I was brought back from my musing when I heard Ed say, "Now that we're in New Orleans, let's see if we can find Joe. Afterwards, we'll settle in at that park we went to before."

"Good," said Jake. We rumbled on down the road until he said, "Go west on that next street. We'll need to drive a ways, but that's the road to take."

My case was now a prison. I wanted to watch as we neared the house, but with little choice to do otherwise, I hunkered down and waited.

After what seemed to be forever, Jake said, "This is it. Turn right on the next road."

I began jumping around in the case.

"Slow down a little, Ed," said Lester. "Things are bumping around back here."

We stopped and someone lifted me out of the van. I heard a knock on the door ... the door opening ...

"Jake! So nice to see you. Everyone come in." Joe's deep resonant voice sent me into orbit. I started fidgeting. *Let me out! Let me out!*

"What brings you here?" asked Joe. "Could it be that you've come to place an order for a guitar?"

I could hear the smile in his voice.

"As a matter of fact, yes," said Jake. "I've reconsidered your offer and would like to have you make that guitar we talked about."

"What made you change your mind?"

"I'll give you a straight answer, Joe. I've become frustrated with this guitar. Something has happened. It doesn't sound as good as it did."

"Really?' said Joe. "That's odd."

Joe would know why I didn't sound as good. He would know how miserable I was, being separated from him. It wasn't odd to him at all. He was playing a game.

"I hope I haven't made you change your mind," said Jake.

"Hmmm. Pull her out and I'll see if I still want her."

I laughed inside. Ha! I knew how badly Joe wanted me. He was having fun with these guys.

The case was opened and Joe picked me up. I was no dummy. I knew the game. If I sounded too good, Jake might want me back. When Joe began to play, I loosened my strings, and the sound I made was terrible.

"I see what you mean, Jake. She sounds awful."

"I'm not sure where we go from here," Jake said. He sounded worried. I could see why. He figured Joe might not want me now. "You said earlier you wanted the guitar as a keepsake because your dad made it for you. Is that offer still good?"

"Possibly, but I'm not sure it's worth me spending hours making one just like it for you." Joe moved an open hand around the workshop, showing the guitars on stands and hanging on the walls. "These are all Marcini guitars, as good as what my father used to make. If you can find one you like, I will give it to you in exchange for this one."

Joe was so smart. He didn't want to have to wait the time it would take to make a guitar. He wanted me now. I started to cross my strings with the hope that Jake wouldn't be too picky. But I caught myself. *I must behave. No antics right now,* I said to myself. *Just act like a stupid, dead-sounding guitar, nothing more.*

Jake moved around the workshop, trying out the different guitars. His face lit up as he strummed a beautiful rosewood one.

"You have a good ear, Jake," said Joe. "That is one of my best guitars."

That's right, Joe. Butter him up.

"I can see how well-made it is," said Jake. "Besides being beautiful, it has an exquisite tone. If your offer is still good, this is the guitar I want in exchange."

"It's yours," said Joe. "And thank you. For sentimental reasons, I'm happy to have the guitar my dad made for me."

Just like that, the deal was made. Jake chose a case, put his new guitar inside, they all shook hands, and The Garma Boys went out the door. I hoped I wasn't dreaming.

🎼 🎵 Chapter 24

"Emma!" Joe yelled. "Come see what I have."

Emma hurried down the stairs. She was much older, but still beautiful, her hair shorter and streaked with gray.

"It's Rose!" she exclaimed. "How did you manage?"

Joe began laughing. "Rose is so clever."

Emma looked perplexed.

"She has been acting up. She made herself sound awful and Jake didn't want her any more."

"Really?"

"Yes. This is a great story, Emma. After telling me how bad Rose sounded, Jake was worried I wouldn't take her back. I acted wary as I took her out of the case. If, when I played her, she'd sounded great, the bluff would have ended, but this clever guitar knew the game. Right on cue, when I strummed a few chords, she sounded horrible."

"But what if something has happened to her and she really isn't the guitar she used to be?"

"I know this guitar well, Emma. I will play something, and you decide."

He smiled, gently took me in his arms, looked at me with his soft, loving eyes, and walked me over to a chair in front of the fireplace. I could see he was not one bit worried about the quality of my sound.

"Rose and I have circled back to the place I had my first guitar lesson." He gave a short laugh. "Prepare yourself for a surprise, Emma."

Joe's eyes twinkled. Still wondering if I was dreaming, I felt my whole self twinkling back. I waited with eager anticipation for Joe to touch my strings.

He began playing a few simple chords. *Ah! Ooh! Ooh! Oh!* I sounded and felt wonderful, amazing, terrific! I hoped I wouldn't explode with happiness. As Joe began to warm up, adding more and more variations to a single theme, I could tell his fingers were not as nimble as they once were, but we formed a balance because with my aging, his fingers brought about a richer sound. I had Joe's back. Whatever he lacked, I would make up for.

Emma clapped and said, "How is it possible? Are you sure she sounded awful just minutes ago? What you just played was beautiful. I don't understand."

Joe didn't break the rhythm to answer. He continued to play and soon we were lost in ourselves. On and on we went, losing track of time, the music swirling and vibrating, filling the room with sounds not heard in this house for many years. I noticed tears running down Emma's cheeks. Her presence as our only audience meant more to me than a Carnegie Hall crowd.

I don't remember her leaving the workshop, but much later Emma called from the door, "Your dinner is getting cold, Joe."

Joe ended the song and carefully set me on a nearby stand.

"We make crazy-wonderful music together, Rose. I've missed you terribly. Welcome home."

His older body seemed light and bouncy as he climbed the steps and went through the door to dinner.